DEATH BY DANCING

A HIGGINS & HAWKE MYSTERY
BOOK FOUR

LEE STRAUSS

la
plume
PRESS

Death by Dancing

© 2021 Lee Strauss

Cover by Jordan Strauss

Cover Illustration by Tasia Strauss

Library and Archives Canada Cataloguing in Publication

Title: Death by Dancing / Lee Strauss.

Names: Strauss, Lee (Novelist), author.

Description: Series statement: A Higgins & Hawke mystery ; 4 | "A 1930s cozy murder mystery."

Identifiers: Canadiana (print) 20210194928 | Canadiana (ebook) 20210194936 | ISBN 9781774091715 (hardcover) | ISBN 9781774091692 (softcover) | ISBN 9781774091708 (IngramSpark softcover) | ISBN 9781774091722 (Kindle) | ISBN 9781774091739 (EPUB) ISBN 978-1-77409-288-0 (bookvault) |ISBN: 978-1-77409-456-3 d2d)

Classification: LCC PS8637.T739 D433 2021 | DDC C813/.6—dc23

THE HIGGINS & HAWKE MYSTERIES

IN ORDER

Death at the Tavern
Death on the Tower
Death on Hanover
Death by Dancing
Death on Tremont Row

*D*r. Haley Higgins could hardly believe she'd been given the esteemed title of Chief Medical Examiner in Boston. There was, however, a little resistance from the mayor and other powers who didn't relish a forty-year-old woman taking the helm of the morgue.

Her predecessor, Dr. Peter Guthrie, had made it his mission to fight on her behalf. He championed her, Haley suspected, not only because she was qualified but because he'd married her maid. After whisking her faithful helper and friend away, Haley imagined her former boss felt he owed her something. And Haley agreed. Molly was an expert cook and housekeeper and quite missed.

Ultimately, if not reluctantly, the mayor and the

chief of police had relented. Haley's work both in medicine and in the way she'd successfully helped the police, inspired Detective Emmet Cluney to not only rally for her, but also put her first in the line of possibilities. Even though feminism had a long way to go, it had made *some* progress. The mayor gave her the position with caveats, and Haley was sure a man in her position would never have been challenged as she was.

Haley grinned to herself as she sat at her former boss' desk and stared through the glass window that looked out onto the morgue, where Dr. Thomas Martin, her young assistant, finished sewing up the Y incision of the male she'd just completed a post-mortem on. An examination of the brain tissue, cut in paper-thin slices, confirmed the brain aneurysm the man's family doctor had suspected. The body would be shuttled to Oakley Funeral Home by the end of the day.

Since Dr. Martin was occupied, Haley answered the telephone when it rang. The morgue benefited from two of those contraptions: an older model hung on the wall by the two desks in the morgue and this more recent tabletop edition.

"City of Boston morgue," Haley said. "Dr. Higgins speaking."

"Dr. 'Iggins!" A thick English accent reminiscent of Dr. Guthrie's greeted her. "I 'ope I'm not botherin' yer."

"Of course not, Mr. Oakley. What can I do for you?"

"Well, it's this body that's come in. Two days ago —one of those marathon dancers. Mrs. Oakley and I've been rather busy of late, and well, we've only just got to it."

Haley pictured Mr. Oakley seated at his desk in a small office at Oakley Funeral Home. Haley's job often put her in the pathway of the local embalmer. In this case, a couple, too jolly to suit their chosen profession.

"Is there a problem with the body, Mr. Oakley?"

"Certainly not to look at 'im, but, well, Dr. 'Iggins it's 'is breath."

"His breath?"

"Yes, well, not 'is breath, exactly, since 'e's not breathin', but you know 'ow slack the jaw gets, and 'ow the mouth just gapes open."

Haley knew the phenomenon, which required creative stitch work by the embalmer when getting the body presentable for viewing.

"What did the odor from the mouth smell like?"

"Well, Mrs. Oakley says carrot, and she should know, 'avin' tended the garden most of 'er life."

Since Mr. Oakley wasn't there to see her, Haley allowed herself to smile broadly at the friendly man. Still, the embalmer's concern over the corpse's "breath" was a reason to take note. "Perhaps I should have a look at the body before you and Mrs. Oakley proceed with embalming."

"That's exactly why I rang you. I shall arrange a driver to drop it off. Will you be at the morgue in the next hour?"

Haley reassured Mr. Oakley she would wait for the delivery. It wasn't like she had anything planned for the evening.

When Haley hung up, Dr. Martin stood in the doorway, drying his hands with a tea towel. Slender and earnest, Thomas Martin looked younger than his twenty-seven years.

"If you're not needing me, Dr. Higgins, would you mind if I left a little early?"

Haley couldn't keep the note of disdain from her voice. "Another spot of duty at the dance marathon?"

"I know you don't like it, Doc, but it's happening just the same."

Haley hated those infernal dance marathons. This one had been running for over three weeks!

With only a few ten-to-fifteen-minute sleep breaks, contestants danced the entire time. Not only was this terribly hard on a person's overall health, but some also didn't survive it, dropping to their death because of cardiac strain, or taking their own lives when they failed to win the big cash prize. That people paid to witness such human abuse made Haley's stomach turn.

But, if those poor souls insisted on putting their bodies through this torture, then medical supervision was a must. Dr. Martin, who'd recently finished medical school, took his turn, and at this stage of the marathon, plenty of doctors and assistants had stepped in.

Except for Haley.

Haley pushed away the guilt that whispered at her. She was giving her time to the dancers when they came into her morgue, like the one headed there now.

"Did you want to come along?" Dr. Martin asked, apparently mistaking her silence as a desire for an invitation. "It really is a sight to behold."

"That's quite all right," Haley said. Out of curiosity, she'd gone on an evening to a dance marathon once before, and that had been enough for her. "A body's coming in, one of those dancers, apparently. Dropped from exhaustion. You can tell me all about it during the postmortem."

"Sure thing, Doctor." As Dr. Martin left, he made an unnecessary, impromptu tap-dance move that could have put Hal Le Roy to shame. She envied his youth.

Speaking of youth, Haley stretched as she stood, her long spine cracking in protest or appreciation; she wasn't sure. Her runaway curls were escaping the knot she'd wrestled her hair into that morning, and she pushed the rebels behind her ears. She noticed that more than a few had turned gray, but there was nothing that a good hat couldn't conceal.

Stepping into the morgue, Haley was pleased to see that Dr. Martin had cleaned things up nicely. Though in the hospital's basement, the morgue was painted a bright white and had good electrical lighting. Outfitted with the latest forensic equipment, including a row of refrigerated cabinets to store the bodies, the room contained a ceramic surgical table, which sat empty and scrubbed clean in the middle of the room. Shelves containing test tubes, Bunsen burners, and tissue samples lined the walls. Two desks sat near the entrance—one occupied by Dr. Martin. Haley's office was behind a glass wall with the benefit of a door to oversee what was happening in the surgery.

The bell that sounded when a body was being delivered through the basement-level door rang. Soon, two men pushed a gurney with the sheet-covered body into the morgue.

The man who backed in said, "Where do you want it, Doc?"

Haley waved a long, thin arm toward the table situated under a large electric lamp. "On the table, if you don't mind." Haley knew how to move a dead body on her own, but why put her own body through the exertion when two strapping men were there to do the task for her?

Haley washed her hands and slipped on a white laboratory coat. She waited until the funeral home men left, wishing them a good evening. She then approached the body.

Clearly male and Caucasian, the body had a tag on his right big toe that read Patrick Baines, along with the date of his death. As Mr. Oakley had said, the corpse's mouth was gaping open. Haley didn't have to get close before she could smell the odor that had caused the embalmer concern.

Haley was fairly certain she was looking at a victim of homicide.

2

*S*amantha Hawke stopped on the busy sidewalk on Water Street and gazed up at the tall, narrow redbrick building that housed *The Boston Daily Record*. Newspaper row was always busy first thing in the morning, and several businessmen dressed in hats and gabardine overcoats had to sidestep past her. She could hear their mutters of annoyance, but she didn't care. A wry smile tugged at the corner of her mouth. Let them get used to making room for her.

Slipping a compact mirror from her purse, she took a quick moment to check her makeup and hair, seeing her breath in the cool March morning. She'd styled her natural blond locks in a long pageboy, smoothly brushed and carefully curled under, topped with a knit beret pulled low over the ears. She went easy with mascara during the daytime hours but could never deny herself her signature dark lipstick. She'd rationed many personal items as the Depression continued, but the lipstick was something she couldn't bring herself to give up. She added a thin layer of red to her lips, gave them a good smack, then walked inside like she owned the place. She'd worked for Archie August for a few years now —while her husband was missing and presumed dead—and she was grateful for the job. Most women had had to vacate their positions to men desperate for the same work.

But that didn't mean her time with the paper had been smooth sailing, far from it, which was why it had become a ritual for her to stop in front of the building every morning and take a deep breath before plunging into the fray.

Passing by a new receptionist—the previous one had recently married—Sam skipped up the steps to the second floor and entered the "pit." The large open room, hazy with smoke from a multitude of partially consumed cigarettes, buzzed with type-writers clacking, loud one-sided telephone conversations, and the intermittent purring of the telegraph spitting out the latest from the Associated Press.

Arranged in tight rows, each desk had its own upright Remington typewriter. Most desks also had dirty ashtrays, stacks of old newspapers, unwashed coffee mugs, and assorted broken pencils.

Besides being the only woman in a roomful of reporters, sportswriters, columnists, and editors, Sam seemed to be the only one who didn't smoke like a chimney. She looked down at the outfit she'd put on that morning—a slim-cut pleated skirt that landed mid-shin, which was coupled with a form-fitting knit sweater detailed with two rows of round buttons and long contrasting knitted cuffs and waistband. She shook her head in annoyance. Why did she even bother trying to get the smell out of her clothes on laundry day?

Samantha made her way to her desk, and after stowing her purse and messenger bag, she lowered herself into her chair and sighed. Her assignment was another fluff piece for the Ladies' Section, this one entitled "Pretty Ideas for House and Home." She wrote on thrilling topics such as ideas for countertop flower arrangements, exciting new wallpaper patterns, modern window dressings—the dreams of most women.

It wasn't like she hadn't proven herself up for the meatier stories. Only two days earlier, when she was an onlooker at the dance marathon, she'd witnessed a spectacle that caused several couples to collapse and become disqualified. She was there to support her good friend Gladys North and husband, Regis. Regis had created quite a stir when one of the male dancers dropped to the floor and became unresponsive. He pushed his wife away and scooped up the fallen man's partner.

Gladys was livid, and Samantha shared her fury until she discovered that Gladys was expecting a baby. She'd conceived just before the marathon had begun but hadn't told Regis until they were well into it; news that made her husband even more determined to win the thousand-dollar prize.

To sportswriter Freddy Hall's dismay, Samantha had scooped the story, and Mr. August had printed it using her byline, Sam Hawke. And yet, despite that victory, here she sat, trying to think of creative ways to discuss spring floral arrangements.

"I'll be sure and ratchet up the suspense on this one," she said out loud, knowing that no one would pay attention, anyway. Even Freddy Hall, intent on his typewriter, hadn't bothered to give her his usual morning glower.

"When do I get to cook a story with real meat in

it instead of only small potato stuff?" she said aloud again as she finally leaned into her typewriter.

This time, someone heard her.

"Hey, doll, that's an old song I hear ya singing."

With dark, oiled hair, Johnny Milwaukee smiled at her as he put down his leather satchel and removed his hat. Though not classically handsome, he possessed a quality—a suave charisma—that made women sit up and pay attention.

With his trademark devil-may-care casualness, Johnny sauntered over and sat on the edge of Samantha's desk, a move which he seemed to be getting very adept at these days. Not that Samantha minded so much. When she started at the paper, he had taken the same adversarial approach that most men used—meaning resentment at having to tolerate a woman in their hallowed workplace. With Johnny, though, it had a flirtatious tone.

Sam had been a widow for six months now, but she wasn't sure how to navigate her relationship with Johnny Milwaukee, a known ladies' man. She had to admit it did make the workplace less dreary though.

"I know, I know," Samantha returned with a half smile. "But six months ago, I helped break a big story and was instrumental in solving a murder. *That's* a big deal, Johnny!"

"It is!" Johnny cocked his chin sideways.

"I appreciate the raise Mr. August gave me, but . . . here I sit. Still locked up in fluff-piece dungeon." She gestured at her typewriter in frustration. "I'm still not taken seriously."

Johnny nodded in somber agreement, but Samantha could see he was struggling to keep a straight face.

"Small-time swamp," he said, raising his eyebrows.

"Paltry prison." Samantha looked away from him to hide her smile tugging at the corners of her mouth. Why was it often so difficult to maintain a proper sour mood with him around?

"Hawke!" Mr. August bellowed at Sam from the open door of his office. "Forget what you're working on for now and get in here."

Samantha and Johnny shared a look as she rose to her feet. Was the tide for her about to change?

"Hall says he's had enough of this darn-tootin' dance marathon." Mr. August, a balding man in his fifties who always had the appearance that he'd just overeaten, his stomach bloating, held his fist at his mouth as he held in a belch. He pushed a piece of paper toward her. "I don't think he's the right guy for the job, anyway. God knows that cement mixer doesn't know the first thing about this kind of stuff. I got Milwaukee on it already, but I think—" he gave her a rare glance of appreciation. "After your story on the last scandal to come from the hall, I think you're the better reporter for it, anyway."

"Hey!"

Samantha glanced over her shoulder at Johnny, who leaned on the doorframe of the editor's office.

Mr. August waved a pudgy hand. "The both of you can cover it. Hawke knows one contestant personally, right?"

Samantha nodded. "Regis North. I'm friends with his wife, Gladys."

"Right, the woman he pushed off the floor." Mr. August's eyes squinted in his round face. "Dumb thing to do, ain't it. If he wins with this new woman, he only gets half the prize."

"Gladys is in the family way," Samantha explained. "Regis didn't know about it when the marathon started. Then he did what he felt was best for his wife."

"I'd do the same thing," Johnny said. "Those dances are brutal. Not fit for a lady expecting a child."

Samantha couldn't agree more.

Mr. August picked up a half-smoked cigar,

trimmed off the end with cigar clippers, and puffed as he lit it. The tip glowed red as the room filled with the aroma of Cuban cigars. After a satisfying release of smoke toward the yellow-tinged ceiling, he said, "Are you in, Hawke? You want the job?"

Samantha's mind reeled at all the things she would need to arrange for her to go out on assignment that night on short notice.

"So, ya want it or not?" Mr. August barked. "I ain't got all day."

Samantha clicked her tongue. "Yes, sir. I'll take it."

3

When Haley finally returned to her fourth-floor apartment on the North End's desirable Grove Street, she expected to find Samantha at home with little Talia tucked into bed.

"Hello?" she called out as she hung her coat on the hook and deposited her hat and gloves on the sideboard by the door.

A quick scan of the living room, kitchen, and bedrooms confirmed her suspicions. She was alone.

Except for Mr. Midnight. The three-legged cat, black as the time of night he was named after, hobbled across the hardwood floor and rubbed his fur against her leg, causing electricity against her stockings. "I wonder what they're up to," she said, leaning down to pat the boy on the head. Mr. Midnight had come to Haley at midnight when Molly still lived and worked for her a few years prior. Molly had captured Haley's former boss's heart, compelling him into early retirement and a life of travel. Initially, Molly had taken Mr. Midnight, but after her honeymoon, she'd asked if Talia would like a pet. After all that the little girl had gone through, losing her father and grandmother in short order, both Haley and Samantha thought the idea was an excellent one.

The kitchen had a brand-new white 1927 General Electric "Monitor Top" refrigerator, with an all-steel cabinet with white walls and sage-green cupboard doors. The size of a large safe, Haley felt fortunate to be able to afford such a useful appliance.

As she'd hoped, Haley found a note on the counter. "Ahh," she said aloud to the cat, who'd hopped onto a wooden chair not pushed to the table. "Sam's on assignment at that dance marathon, and Talia's with Mrs. Berrymaple."

Haley wondered if she should get Talia and save Samantha from waking the amiable Mrs. Berrymaple in the middle of the night. Then again, she'd probably arranged for her daughter to spend the night with their widowed neighbor, who spent more time alone than she preferred.

Instead, Haley turned on the kitchen radio to

dull the silence, then wished she hadn't. With an excited voice, the reporter at the dance marathon gave a play-by-play on the latest endurance test, a couple's race lapping the gymnasium to the finish line. "Mr. And Mrs. Sikes are the couple to beat! Look at 'em go!"

Haley fiddled with a knob until she found a station playing "Life is Just a Bowl of Cherries," then made herself a sandwich with the leftover roasted chicken. Checking if the milk was still cold in the refrigerator, she poured herself a tall glass. Her mind drifted back to the body she'd left behind in the morgue. After notifying Detective Cluney of her suspicions, Haley had scheduled an autopsy for the morning.

Secured to the wall in the kitchen, the boxy wooden telephone unexpectedly rang, and Haley jumped. She brushed her hands on her skirt and pushed her curly hair out of the way before holding the black cup-like receiver to her ear.

"Hello, darling," came a warm and friendly male voice. "I missed you at the theater tonight. I hope everything is all right?"

Haley slapped a hand to her forehead. "Gerald, I'm so sorry. A suspicious death came in at the end of the day—the play completely slipped my mind."

A well-respected geriatrics doctor, Dr. Gerald Mitchell was a recent widower and a long-time friend of Haley's. Now that they were single at the same time, their friendship was slowly turning into something more.

"I expected as much," Gerald said, and Haley was relieved to hear the smile in his voice. She imagined him sitting in his leather armchair in his study, nibbling on a pipe stem, his graying hair oiled and combed off his forehead. "Shall we rebook for tomorrow evening?"

"I'd love that," Haley said, but something stopped her from committing. "Can I let you know tomorrow? I have an autopsy in the morning and may be needed by the police. I'd hate to make a promise I can't keep."

"Very well. Once you know, call me tomorrow or leave a message with Sissy if I'm not around." Sissy was Gerald's charwoman who cleaned for him three times a week.

"I will," Haley said, her eyes reverting to her unfinished sandwich. "As soon as I know."

Gerald ended the call with well-wishes for good sleep, and Haley returned to her food. Her appetite often waned at work, and she was famished when she got home each day. A hot bath and a book crossed her mind, but she couldn't forget about the body in the morgue.

He'd been a dance contestant.

Samantha was reporting on the dance.

Forfeiting her time of leisure, Haley grabbed her coat and hat. She turned to Mr. Midnight, who gazed up, his green eyes narrowing in disapproval.

"So sorry to leave you alone again, Mr. Midnight," she said. "Don't wait up."

4

*S*amantha, weighed down slightly by her oversized purse and camera bag, approached the entrance to the suburban gymnasium. She noticed a new billboard next to the entry kiosk with the slogan, "Stumbling, Staggering, On They Go! Who will be the next to be carried off the floor? Tonight: Derby endurance race!"

Underneath that slogan, in smaller letters, was written, "Twenty-five cents will get you in 'til midnight. One full dollar will let you stay 'til daylight."

"Clever rhyme," Samantha muttered with a nod toward the billboard as she showed the woman at the door her press pass.

"Mr. Farber ain't nuthin' if he ain't clever," the

woman returned. She adjusted her glasses to read the card. "You were here a couple nights ago, paid your two bits, if I remember correctly. Now, you're a reporter?" She lowered her glasses as if wanting a closer look at Samantha, then added with a note of suspicion, "A *woman* reporter?"

"That's right." With a sniff, Samantha reluctantly added, "I'm here with Mr. Milwaukee."

The woman grunted as she handed Samantha back her card, with an unplucked eyebrow raised. "A woman hack, huh? Ain't that rich. Well, Mr. Milwaukee is already inside." She waved down the hall to the gymnasium entrance door.

The place was packed—even more crowded than two nights before. The bleacher section, which extended the entire circumference of the oval around the wooden dance floor, was packed. Samantha estimated at least fifteen hundred people, many of them women, watched the somnambulant contestants swaying back and forth below them.

And with them, the smell. Samantha held a gloved hand over her nose, having learned from the last time it took about ten minutes to become desensitized to the body odor.

Red, white, and blue cloth streamers hung along the metal railings that separated the bleacher section from the dance floor and looked rather droopy after so much time in a warm and humid room. If the decor and the contestants looked tired, the energy that accompanied the crowd that evening was full of bottled-up expectancy. There was a gladiator-type hunger for blood sport, and the endurance test scheduled for that evening would be torturous for the bone-tired contestants. Samantha did not doubt that more couples would be eliminated that night. The question was who?

The reigning champions, the married couple named Sikes, were the crowd's favorite to win, and this prospect kept the local bookies busy. Regis North was holding up his new partner, Bernice Prescott, whose former partner had inexplicably collapsed two nights previous.

Gladys watched from the sidelines, her eyes sunken with dark circles and her small mouth pinched. Having long ago lost its curls, her short brown hair hung in strands framing a thin face. Despite being off the dance floor, her friend clearly hadn't been sleeping. Samantha waved a hand, catching Gladys's attention. Her friend waved back, then returned her focus to her husband.

A man wearing a tuxedo, his hair slicked back, and his tie loose, sat at a piano, playing as if he were entertaining wealthy patrons at an elite lounge instead of a smelly gymnasium. He crooned into a microphone,

"You must remember this,
a kiss is still a kiss,
a sigh is just a sigh.
The fundamental things apply
as time goes by."

"Hey, doll." Johnny Milwaukee got up from his seat near the bottom of the bleacher section and strolled over. He lifted a bristle-shadowed chin at Mr. Owen, indicated the photographer should follow, then strolled over with his fists stuffed in his trouser pockets.

"How many left?" Samantha asked.

"Nineteen couples," Johnny said. "That makes one hundred and six couples who have dropped out."

"I see that Regis North and Bernice Prescott have been allowed to continue together. When I wrote the story, the validity of Regis's move was in hot debate."

Johnny reached into his jacket pocket and produced a cigarette. "The judges ruled that, since Miss Prescott didn't stop moving her feet even as her partner let go of her and collapsed, she hadn't disqualified herself."

"She must have just kept moving her feet out of reflex," Samantha mused.

"North was as quick as a cat to jump in," Johnny said, "grabbing Miss Prescott by the waist and whisking her off."

Samantha recalled the event. "They carted off poor Patrick Baines with a horrified Bernice Prescott looking over the shoulder of her new partner."

After lighting his cigarette, Johnny said, "It's like some kinda movie or somethin'. You got romance, survival, danger . . ."

"Look at that couple." Samantha pointed. "She's fast asleep."

The young man in question had his eyes closed as he swayed back and forth and carried the full weight of his partner, who wore a blue cotton dress covered in white polka dots. Her hands were tied with a handkerchief around the back of his neck, and her feet were tied to the top of his.

"They must've done that during the last break," Johnny said. "Apparently, it's normal this far into it. They take turns sleeping on each other."

Samantha's gaze darted back to Gladys. Even in extreme exhaustion, Regis had been quick on his feet, his mind recognizing an opportunity and snatching it as if by reflex. Sam was grateful for the sake of her weary friend.

Johnny flicked his wrist and stared at his watch. "The Kentucky Derby-style race is going to start pretty soon. That'll eliminate a few more couples."

Samantha wrinkled her nose. The Kentucky Derby was a horse race, where the animals carried extra weight and ran straight out for about two minutes. "Cyril and Thelma Sikes are still going strong, I see," she said.

Johnny blew smoke up toward the ceiling. "They won the last two marathons they entered, and I think they're going to win this one too. Of all the contestants, they have the physical and mental conditioning to go the distance."

"The calendar guy is still going with his partner." Sam pointed to the far side of the dance floor at a couple she'd observed two nights earlier. The man had a small white calendar hanging on his back with the days of the month of the marathon so far X'ed out.

A large timer hung from the ceiling. "The dance has already gone on for over five hundred hours," Samantha said, astounded there was anyone still on the dance floor. "He's had to change that calendar twice and is close to having to change it again."

"When I got here tonight," Johnny said, "his partner had a mirror with a little metal dish attached hanging from her chin so he could shave."

"I'm sorry I missed that," Samantha said.

"Don't worry; he'll do it again tomorrow." Johnny chuckled. "If we're lucky, we'll get to see her put on her makeup."

"That'll boost our readership," Samantha said glibly. "A new twist for the ladies' pages."

Just then, a woman collapsed to her knees while her partner yelled, "No, no, Doris! Stay up! A break is coming!" He tried to hold her weight while a judge, dressed in a suit and tie, ran out from beside a bleacher carrying a ruler in his hand. The contestant bent down and tried, but failed, to lift his partner's dead weight. The official attempted to measure the distance between the woman's knees and the floor, but then her partner dropped her. The judge waved to the sidelines, and another man dressed in white ran over to the collapsed woman. Together, they carried the woman off the floor. Her partner sobbed as he buried his head in his hands.

Even as Samantha wrote the couple's name—printed on the cards tied around their necks—in her notebook, she felt immense pity, feeling slightly ashamed of being a helpless witness to their lost hopes and dreams.

It did make a good story, though.

A horn blasted, and the remaining couples immediately stopped dancing. A door opened on the side of the auditorium, and in a flurry of well-organized precision, thirty-eight army cots were quickly wheeled out onto the floor. All the cots had a contestant's name pinned to the pillow, and each was immediately claimed by an exhausted contestant, who dropped like a sack of potatoes onto their appointed mattress.

Almost every one of them seemed to be asleep instantly, while people streamed down along the aisles from the upper bleachers to get a closer look at the evidence of self-inflicted agony.

Across the gymnasium, through the crowd's ebb and flow, Samantha thought she spotted a tall woman with very curly brown hair.

Haley?

The crowd's movement blocked Samantha's line of sight, and she just shook her head, thinking she must have been mistaken. Haley Higgins would never attend such a barbaric spectacle as this.

Gladys appeared by her husband's side, a busy nurse conceding to let her tend to her husband. She helped Nurse Winkley hand out glasses of water to those who were still awake, and Samantha couldn't help but notice a scathing look that passed between the nurse and Bernice Prescott. What on earth was going on there?

Thelma Sikes's hand shook as she lifted her glass to her mouth, and as bad luck would have it, a competitor knocked into her cot, causing her to drop her glass.

"Watch it, buster!" she called out. "Now my dress is wet!"

Nurse Winkley was quick to provide a new glass. "Here you go, Mrs. Sikes. You don't want to get dehydrated."

Mrs. Sikes gulped back the water, clearly taking the nurse's admonition to heart, and Samantha couldn't help but wonder what drove a woman like her to do such a dangerous and difficult thing as this.

5

The first thing to strike Haley about the dance marathon were the harsh smells of unwashed bodies and nervous anticipation that filled the air. As a pathologist, she was used to body odors, especially the stench of disintegrating flesh. Nonetheless, the first steps into the gymnasium were unpleasant, and her gloved hand went immediately to her face, covering her mouth and nose.

It wasn't the first time Haley had witnessed the dance marathon spectacle, a recent social phenomenon she strongly disapproved of. However, it didn't keep her from paying her quarter. She might admit to a bit of morbid curiosity, but her primary interest was in seeing what Mr. Baines had been exposed to the night he died.

The gymnasium was full of rowdy spectators, smoking, swaying to the music, chatting loudly over each other. Despite this, no dancers were on the floor. Instead, Haley witnessed something more akin to a war triage, the floor lined with cots supporting dancers in a coma-like sleep, dead to the cacophony that continued around them.

She jumped at the sound of a loud megaphone, and immediately dance officials roughly shook the sleepers awake while other assistants crudely stole the cots from underneath them, rolling them through a door at the back. As if in a trance, the dancers found their partners, fell into each other's arms, and defied nature's call for them to rest. Officials were quick to yell orders to keep moving or be disqualified, and more than one couple could not comply. When the knees of the failing partner were measured to be less than six inches off the floor, it was automatic elimination.

Dr. Martin stood by the nurses' station where the newly expelled were checked over before being sent home. Haley pushed her way through the crowd intending to reach him, only to be stopped before she could.

A rotund man with a beaming, insincere smile

held out an oily palm. "Only contestants and officials beyond this point, ma'am."

Haley smiled, hoping to disarm the fellow. "I'm Dr. Higgins, Chief Medical Examiner from the coroner's office. My assistant, Dr. Martin, is volunteering at the nurses' station. And who would you be?"

"Farber." The damp palm took hers, and good manners forced Haley to accept. "Boyd Farber," the man continued. "I'm the organizer of this fine event."

"Yes, well—" Haley attempted to hide her disdain at what was clearly an uncivilized function.

Mr. Farber flashed a horsey smile. "Since you're a doctor, and a lady, and a paying customer?" He raised a bushy brow, and Haley nodded. He continued, "I'll allow you access." He removed a barrier and waved her through. "Enjoy yourself, Dr. Higgins."

Not likely.

"Thank you, Mr. Farber."

Dr. Martin's brow buckled when he saw Haley approach. "Dr. Higgins! What are you doing here?"

"A bit of curiosity has tempted me, Dr. Martin. So much fuss and nonsense, as Dr. Guthrie would've said."

With a glint in his eye, Dr. Martin nodded knowingly. "You're here because of that body."

Haley conceded. "Yes. Patrick Baines had been a contestant."

"Baines?" The voice was high-pitched and came from one of the nurses standing at Dr. Martin's side. "Mr. Patrick Baines? Is he all right? Oh, I do hope so."

Haley turned to the nurse, a competent-looking woman in her mid-twenties, and said, "I'm Dr. Higgins."

Dr. Martin added, "Dr. Higgins, this is Nurse Mildred Winkley. She's heading up the nursing station."

Haley and Nurse Winkley exchanged hellos, then Haley asked. "How do you know Mr. Baines?"

Nurse Winkley sneered. "Only from this baloney. A bunch of them dropped like flies after the last endurance test. He stood out to me, looking poorly." She grimaced as her focus skimmed the dance floor. "I can hardly imagine how this bunch is going to survive tonight's test."

Haley hoped the nurse's use of the word "survive" was hyperbole. "What's the test?"

"A sprint," Dr. Martin said. "Like the Olympics, only as pairs."

Nurse Winkley sniffed. "More like horses being beaten as they go to the slaughterhouse."

The nurse seemed not to like her position at the dance marathon, but money was money, and Haley knew that even skilled professionals hadn't been spared hardship from the stock market collapse. She'd been fortunate that she'd decided to pull her money out of the markets in the summer of '29. Because of that, she found herself a member of the *haves*, instead of the *have nots*, and with this ongoing depression, there didn't seem to be many people in between.

Nurse Winkley was called away, and Haley was left with Dr. Martin. "I know I'm preaching to the choir," she said, "but I agree with Nurse Winkley's sentiments. This is brutish. This level of exhaustion is not only incredibly unhealthy, but it's also inhumane."

"A thousand dollars is a lot of money to these people," Dr. Martin said. "Desperate times, as they say."

Haley couldn't deny the desperation in the air. "These poor people are like rag dolls, barely holding their partners up, much less themselves. And now, they're going to make them race?"

Dr. Martin snorted. "It thins the herd. And brings people in to watch. More people mean more money."

"For whom?" Haley demanded.

Dr. Martin pointed to Mr. Farber. "Him, mostly. But the city cashes in as well."

The pianist moved from one tune to the next, but this time, dance officials corralled the contestants to the middle of the room.

"They're setting up for the endurance test," Dr. Martin said.

The repositioning of the people created an opening for Haley to see the spectators on the other side of the floor. A special box had been designated for the press, and Haley recognized her roommate, chatting with her colleague Mr. Milwaukee. Haley smirked as she watched the couple banter. The two were clearly attracted to each other, even though they both did what they could to deny it. Haley wasn't sure why. None of her business, though. She attempted to catch Samantha's eye, preparing to offer a wave, but Mr. Milwaukee had Sam's rapt attention.

The contestants were pushed to a starting line, the music unrelenting and the dancers forever swaying. Haley watched the games like a spectator at an ancient coliseum, waiting for the lions to be released. She jumped when the horn blasted. The race was on.

. . .

SAMANTHA LEANED into Johnny and shouted over the cheering crowd. "I'm going to talk to Gladys North." Her inference was that readers might be interested in how the discarded wife felt, but she honestly wanted to make sure her friend was all right.

She found her in the same spot as before, high on the bleacher, scowling at her husband, with Bernice Prescott's limp form draped around him.

"Tough break," Samantha said, sitting beside her. "But if Regis goes the distance, you still get the prize money," Samantha reminded her.

"Yeah, but only half. We lost five hundred clams the moment he threw me aside."

"But you'll keep five hundred. Think about your health and your baby too."

Gladys's frown lines were deeply etched as she ran a palm over her stomach. "A lot of good it's goin' to do if we can't afford to feed it."

"You know, they actually banned these types of marathons in Washington last year," Samantha said. "Tacoma and Seattle."

Gladys spared Samantha a glance. "The City of Boston, too, but not the suburbs."

A loophole of which Mr. Farber had taken advantage. Samantha pressed her point. "A Seattle woman tried to commit suicide when she didn't make it to the end."

"She shouldn't have entered then," Gladys said. "This contest isn't for the weak."

Samantha couldn't keep the shock at hearing her friend's lack of sympathy from reaching her face. She felt her cheeks flush with heat.

Gladys reached down and unbuckled her shoes, tossed them to the side, and worked out the toes of her very blistered feet. "I'm not trying to be mean, Sam. It's just the truth. And I'm just so steamed at Regis. I don't enjoy watching him out there dancing with another woman. It doesn't feel right."

"I'm sure Regis has your best interest at heart. It's not like he wanted this to happen. I don't think Bernice Prescott wanted it to happen either."

"I know, I know."

The air horn sounded, announcing the beginning of the next round. As the piano man played another song, the hefty organizer jumped awkwardly onto the stage and yelled through a giant blue-and-white megaphone like a circus barker. "Who's going to be next to drop?"

Max Owen, the shy newspaper photographer on Johnny's heels, followed the Sikeses couple around the floor, asking them to pose for *The Boston Daily*

Record. Mr. Farber strutted about, barking orders at officials who looked to be taking things in a little too leisurely. Reaching into his pocket, Mr. Farber tossed a few coins onto the dance floor, then shouted, "Don't forget to encourage your favorite couple!" Cyril and Thelma Sikes reached down to pick them up, all the while with their feet still moving.

"It's the joy of victory or the agony of de-feet!" Mr. Farber chortled, laughing heartily at his own pun.

Samantha frowned at the man's antics, already planning to write him into her piece under an ill light.

Mr. Farber continued with his glee-filled instructions. "Okay, we need all the dancers to move closer together into the middle while we get the oval track marked out onto the floor with painter's tape."

A cheer went up from the crowd. Many spectators held up signs declaring, "Our dime, your time!" and "Don't turn off the lights 'til the prize belongs to Sikes."

The floor judges marked out a crude inner oval the circumference of the floor, effectively making a racetrack about fifteen feet wide the whole way around it. The entire time they worked with measuring sticks and tape, Boyd Farber continued to prime the crowd while the pianist pounded out snappy tunes. The pianist was soon joined by a man playing a marching drum, two trumpet players, and someone playing the double bass. Between the loud music and the noise of the exuberant crowd, Samantha could barely think straight. She rubbed the back of her neck where a headache threatened to take over.

The music suddenly ended as Boyd Farber spit into his megaphone. "And *nooow,* ladies and gentlemen, you're about to witness ten minutes of prancing, dancing, running, and stumbling on our specially constructed track." At this, there was a roar of laughter from the crowd as he pointed to the tape markings on the floor. Waving his free arm wildly, he continued, "You are about to witness a great extravaganza, youza, youza! Who will set the pace? Who will win the race?" He pointed a thick finger up at the counter hanging from the ceiling. "Over five hundred and four hours on the clock, but at the end of these next ten minutes, many couples will drop out of the dance! Citizens of Boston, I give you . . . Derby!"

At that, the band struck up again in a frenzied tune, and all the dancing contestants, running side by side with their partners, started what could only be described as a fast shuffle around the track. No one was running; it was rather more like walking at speed. With looks of pain and effort on their faces, tired couples made their way around the track as the crowd roared.

After a few laps, the favored couple to win, Cyril and Thelma Sikes, had taken a narrow lead, with Regis North and Bernice Prescott closing in. The rest of the couples grouped in behind them.

It didn't take long before many dancers dropped to the ground. Floor judges raced over, counting down as if it were a boxing match. The panicked partners yelled manically at their fallen, and to Samantha's horror, one kicked a prone man in the back. At the end of the ten-count, the collapsed dancers were dragged off the track, their distraught partners shuffling behind.

Samantha wrote furiously on her notepad to find descriptive words that would help her later describe the bedlam.

Brutal, shocking, deafening, savage, inhumane.

Samantha's shoulders sank. Sometimes the English language was woefully inept.

6

*H*aley gripped the collar of her blouse, furious that she could witness humanity being entertained by the blatant suffering of others in these modern times. And for what reason? Because of poor economic management at every level of government.

After their short rest break, the couple, now known as North and Prescott, struggled around the first corner. A man cupped his mouth, created a makeshift blow horn, and shouted, "C'mon, North! Give us something to get excited about!"

Miss Prescott winced in pain, and Haley marveled at the stamina of the young woman. Despite Haley's surge of adrenaline from witnessing this spectacle, she fought fatigue—she'd been on her feet and working all day—and that was with having a whole night's sleep!

Years of medical school had informed her on the science of sleep and its importance to the proper function of the systems in the human body. These people could do irreparable damage, easily shortening their lives, and all to claim a monetary prize and fifteen minutes of fame.

How had this great country come to this? Americans treated worse than racehorses.

As Mr. Farber had intended, the "herd" thinned as couple after couple dropped to the floor, the unconscious one being dragged off by men dressed in white, while the partner wailed in disappointment.

Haley sympathized with their grief. For most, it meant a return to life with little food and possibly no roof over their heads.

Cyril and Thelma Sikes had moved to the front of the pack, with Regis North and Bernice Prescott not far behind and gaining fast. Two other couples were neck and neck for the third spot. Haley held her breath, waiting for the ten-minute endurance test to end.

With thirty seconds to go and on the last lap, a ribbon was strung across the far section of the track as the crowd's roar grew even louder. Moments later, Cyril and Thelma Sikes crossed the ribbon first, with Regis North and Bernice Prescott just one step behind.

Absolute pandemonium broke out from the bleachers, forcing Haley to cover her ears. As a doctor, she understood how sensitive the ear drum was, and she, for one, wished to continue to hear properly into her old age.

Just as the roar of celebration reached a crescendo, a collective gasp blanketed the crowd. Before the cots were brought out for another ten-minute rest, Bernice Prescott collapsed in the far-backside of the gym.

Regis North was having none of that and quickly pulled his partner upright and pressed her against his body. He slapped her face. Haley saw his mouth move as he shouted, "Snap out of it, Bernice! I'll not let you ruin this for me!"

Haley watched with consternation. Bernice Prescott failed to respond to her partner's abuse, hanging in his arms like a rag doll.

"Bernice!" Mr. North's enraged voice reached the rafters; even so, Miss Prescott failed to respond. Nurse Winkley and Dr. Martin ran to assist, but Mr. North held out a palm. "No! She's fine."

Even without a doctorate, Haley would have known that Miss Prescott was, in fact, not fine. She ducked under the tape and ran to Dr. Martin's side.

"Mr. North," she said with authority. "I'm Dr. Higgins. I'm going to check Miss Prescott's vitals."

"Fine," he said with vinegar, his feet dragging back and forth like his shoes were lined with lead. Heartlessly, a break wasn't scheduled for immediately after the Derby, and the poor souls had to keep moving. "But for the record judges," Mr. North continued, "we're still dancing."

Haley nodded to appease the man, then placed two fingers on Miss Prescott's neck, swaying along with Mr. North to keep her fingers in place. The woman's lips had turned blue, so Haley wasn't surprised when she didn't find a pulse. She glanced at Dr. Martin and gave a subtle shake of her head.

Turning back to Regis North, she said gently, "Mr. North, I'm afraid your dancing partner has passed away."

Regis North's mouth gaped open, his bloodshot eyes blinking as he registered the information. His feet finally stopped as shock took over. He lifted his arms, pushing the dead body away. Thankfully, Dr. Martin was ready and caught the corpse before it crumpled to the floor.

"Haley! It *is* you."

Haley turned to Samantha's familiar voice. "Sam," she said, then leaned to speak into her friend's ear. "I'm afraid Miss Prescott has died."

Samantha's blue eyes widened with alarm. "Oh no. Poor thing!"

Her head turned to Regis North and then to the bleachers where his wife sat looking stricken. "I guess that's the end of Gladys's hope," she said.

Haley nodded. "I'm afraid so."

An official pushed a rolling cot to where they were gathered, prepared to whisk away another contestant he assumed had simply passed out.

"I wish I'd brought my bag," Haley said. Normally she was called to the scene after the body had been discovered by someone else. She did what she could to examine the body, presuming, at first, Miss Prescott had died due to complications tied to exhaustion. Perhaps she'd been born with a weak heart or experienced organ trauma because of dehydration and lack of blood circulation.

It was only when she got a whiff of the smell that came from Miss Prescott's open mouth that Haley gave pause.

Oddly, it smelled of carrot, like that of the corpse of Mr. Baines, Miss Prescott's former dance partner.

The coincidence was too much to ignore.

"Dr. Martin," Haley called.

Her assistant came immediately. "Yes, Doc?"

"There must be a telephone in this building somewhere. Track it down and call the police."

amantha locked eyes with Haley for an intense moment.

Haley's wide jaw tightened. "I'm afraid your story has suddenly changed its scope."

"Meaning?"

"Cause of death."

Samantha inquired, "Not a heart attack?"

Haley stared at her with meaning. "Poison."

Samantha stilled, her pen pausing over the page. No guff, this story had changed scope! Recovering from her initial surprise, she scratched her pencil across her notepad rapidly. Preparing her Kodak box camera, she was thankful that the lighting over the dancers was especially bright. "Haley, you don't mind?"

"Only if you promise to share them with me before you publish them."

"Of course."

"Concentrate on the chest and facial area, but also get some shots of the way the body is lying on the floor."

Keeping her eye on Johnny, who'd moved to the next couple holding each other up as if for dear life, Samantha snapped the photos. She finished just as Johnny flipped his notebook shut and started toward her, frowning at the sight of Miss Prescott's body still lying on the back corner of the dance floor.

Mr. Farber bolted over. "Why is she still here?"

Before he could yell for more dance officials, Haley held up a palm. "Mr. Farber, I regret to inform you that this young lady has died."

Mr. Farber stared at Haley as if she'd just spoken to him in a foreign language, his thick eyelids slowly blinking, his lips falling open. Samantha kept her pen at the ready, eager to capture the exchange.

"Well," he finally managed. "It happens. The dancers know the risks before they join up." He poked his temple with a stubby finger. "I make them sign a waiver. Johnson!"

The official sprinted over at his boss' command, but Haley once again raised a palm.

"Mr. Farber, I must inform you of the seriousness of this situation. I can't let you move the body."

"Why in the heat of hades not?"

"Because I believe this woman's been murdered. The police have been called."

"You can't bloody well leave her here with the dancers moving around her."

Samantha shared a look with Haley. If poison had caused death, moving the body to another room wouldn't compromise evidence.

Haley responded to Mr. Farber. "Very well." Then she instructed the dance attendants, "Please move her into the nurses' station."

As Samantha continued to scribble in her notepad, Mr. Farber flapped his hands in her face.

"No, no, we need to keep this out of the press for the moment. Miss—"

Samantha filled in the blank. "Hawke, Miss Hawke."

With round eyes, he implored her, "Miss Hawke, can't you wait until this is all over? We are nearing the end, anyway." To Haley, he chose a childlike whine, "Dr. Higgins . . ."

Samantha and Haley looked at the remaining dancers on the floor, all weak yet with finish-line determination registered on their faces.

"It seems to me the marathon could go on for several more hours," Haley said. "Perhaps days." She stared at the organizer with authority. "I'm afraid you have until the police arrive. Then it's up to the leading investigator whether you will have to shut your business down."

With a string of blue cuss words, Mr. Farber stormed away, seemingly forgetting his recent plea to Sam.

Samantha glanced at Johnny Milwaukee, who'd wasted no time approaching Cyril and Thelma Sikes to get their reaction, and beating her to the punch, Mr. Owen's flash popping as he took photographs.

Should she tell Johnny that Bernice Prescott was dead? Or should she scoop him?

She had only seconds to decide.

Haley's voice pulled her to the present. "You'll give me copies of the negatives?"

"What?"

Haley pointed to her camera. "The negatives."

"Ah, yes."

"And you won't publish them?"

"No, not until after you and the police give the okay. Um—Haley, I'll be back in a jiffy. Uh, need the restroom."

With that, Samantha darted away, leaving a

perplexed Johnny Milwaukee stepping next to Haley. Samantha didn't worry that Haley would share her suspicions with Johnny. Except for Samantha, Haley didn't trust the press, her dislike going back to her perceived mistreatment and subsequent poor reporting when her brother Joseph had been murdered.

Samantha grabbed an official and spoke with urgency. "Where might I find the telephone? It's important."

The official gave her easy directions, and when Samantha found the phone, she dialed the operator. "Please connect me to Mr. Archie August at *The Boston Daily Record.*"

HALEY'S RELIEF was enormous when she finally caught sight of Detective Emmet Cluney. A large man with a serious expression, the detective lumbered toward her with two uniformed officers in tow, one of whom she recognized as Officer Tom Bell. Samantha had once confided to Haley that the young officer operated as her police contact occasionally.

Haley waved a long, slim arm. "Detective! Over here."

Detective Cluney's thick neck turned to her voice, and he hollered at the crowd as he pushed through. "Get outta my way. Police. Coming through!"

The cacophony of inharmonious sounds—a disgruntled crowd, a tired band, and Mr. Farber's incessant grumbling—had given Haley a headache. The heat in the gymnasium didn't help, with the sweaty bodies giving off heat. Droplets of sweat formed on the back of her neck, and she lifted her curls with one hand to cool down.

"Detective Cluney," she said as he drew near.

He wrinkled his nose. "What a stink pit. The whole bunch needs to be run through the showers."

Haley had been on the premises so long she no longer noticed the stench of nervous sweat and stale air. However, the waft of cigar smoke the detective had carried in on his jacket was sharp yet pleasant compared with anything else in the room. She led him to the nurses' station, where he stared at the body of Bernice Prescott, lying on one of the cots.

Detective Cluney grunted. "Dispatch says you think we got a homicide here."

"Like everyone else, I thought she'd simply dropped from exhaustion. Dr. Martin, the doctor on standby, and the head nurse came to revive her, but—"

"She was already dead." Detective Cluney sighed. "Got a niece her age. Such a shame." He locked eyes with Haley. "It's not unheard of for the ticker to give out at these affairs, even in the youngsters."

"That occurred to me too . . ." Haley admitted.

"But? Spit it out, Doctor. I told the missus I wouldn't be long."

After working with Detective Cluney for several years, Haley was used to his gruffness and was unruffled by it.

"It's the smell coming from her mouth."

The vertical lines above Detective Cluney's short nose deepened. "She has bad breath? I reckon every soul in this place does too."

"Not bad, per se," Haley said patiently. "A particular scent. I have another body in the morgue, a former contestant named Patrick Baines, who died two nights ago after collapsing. He emitted the same smell."

"I see." Detective Cluney hummed. "You think there's a correlation between the two deaths. Something nefarious."

"I do. They were partners at the beginning of the

contest. When Mr. Baines collapsed, another contestant swooped up his partner, Miss Prescott, before she missed a dance beat."

Detective Cluney rubbed his chin. "And that's allowed? To swap partners in the middle of a marathon? What of his partner?"

"He discarded his pregnant wife for her own good, I imagine," Haley said. "Whether it's allowed is currently being hotly debated."

"What's the smell? Poison?"

"I strongly suspect it to be so. I'd rather wait for laboratory testing before wagering a guess."

Detective Cluney peered out the doorway into the gym, and Haley stared out after him. Four remaining couples continued to sway, though the Sikeses seemed unnaturally energized. Haley wouldn't have been surprised if they were using steroids and wondered if an illegal substance had something to do with her two corpses.

Detective Cluney waved his officers over. "We gotta shut it down."

Officer Bell lifted his chin. "There'll be a riot, sir."

"Oh, dagnabit! Last thing I need is for another death because of a darn-tootin' stampede. But we gotta potential murder to investigate."

"If we can move the body to my morgue," Haley started, "you and your men could begin a covert investigation. Everyone who might be a suspect is probably still here."

Detective Cluney rocked on his shoes as he cupped his chin. "You heard the lady, boys. No one who's part of this operation leaves this gym without speaking to one of us first. There must be another room in the back where you can round 'em up."

A roar from the crowd stole their attention, bringing their focus to the edge of the dance floor. Three of the four couples, like bowling pins, teetered, one partner's dead weight pulling on the other. Seemingly unable to bear the weight of her male partner, a woman cried out. Judges ran with their rulers, measuring the knee-to-floor distance of the two sleeping women whose partners struggled to keep them upright, ensuring that the six-inch rule wasn't broken.

"Out!" One claimed, followed quickly by the disqualification of the other.

In minutes, only Cyril and Thelma Sikes were left standing. Mr. Farber ran to their side, shouting, "The winners, ladies and gentlemen! The winners!"

The Sikeses collapsed into each other's arms. Chairs decorated like royal thrones were pushed to the middle of the floor, and officials helped the winners to the seats. The band played triumphant music as the newspaper cameramen flashed cameras sparking more excitement.

It happened so fast; Haley could barely catch her breath. She couldn't have imagined such a dramatic ending if she'd planned it.

8

*A*fter a rushed breakfast, Samantha walked out the front door of their apartment with Talia at her side. Thankfully, Talia's private school was only a fifteen-minute walk and on a bus route. After dropping her daughter off every morning, Samantha caught the bus to *The Boston Daily Record* on Water Street. They had done it so often that the morning sequence of events had become routine—Talia taking too long to eat her breakfast and then going on like a chatterbox while trying to keep up with her mother's long strides as they walked along the sidewalk.

It was always the highlight of Samantha's day.

She glanced down at her daughter, whose blond locks bounced back and forth as she skipped along with her schoolbooks bound in a leather strap and slung over her shoulder. Samantha was sure Talia was the most beautiful eight-year-old girl in the whole school.

"Tell me one thing you learned yesterday," Samantha chirped. The question was also a daily ritual. It had started one day in first grade when Talia suddenly declared she didn't see the need for school anymore because she had learned everything already.

"I learned that scientists discovered a new planet not too long ago!"

This particular school was known for its excellent science program, for which Talia had already shown considerable aptitude.

"I heard about that."

"Ya, it's tiny, though. At first, they called it Planet X, but then an eleven-year-old girl from England called it Pluto, and the name stuck!" Without skipping a beat, Talia displayed her usual talent for lightning-fast changes of conversation topics. "Can we play snakes and ladders again tonight?"

"I wish I could, but I have to work."

"Aw, nuts!" Talia kicked a rock on the sidewalk.

"But Mrs. B. probably would. Would you like to play with her?"

Talia's countenance saddened.

"What is it?" Samantha asked. "I thought you liked Mrs. Berrymaple?"

"I do. She's very nice, but she reminds me of Bubba. I miss Bubba."

Bina, called Bubba by Talia, had been Samantha's late mother-in-law and the only grandparent Talia had ever known. She had been irritable, judgmental, and a pain in the neck, but she was a good grandmother, stepping in for Samantha when working, much like Mrs. Berrymaple did now.

"I know you miss your grandmother, but did you know that Mrs. B doesn't have any granddaughters? I think you're meant for each other."

Talia considered the logic, smiled, then promptly changed the subject.

"We had peanut butter and tomato soup for lunch yesterday."

Samantha was more than grateful for the school lunch program. She had read that the school districts in some states were so poor they'd had to cut back teachers' salaries and shorten the school year to five months. Some families couldn't even afford textbooks for their children. At Talia's school, meals were usually nutritious and balanced. Talia didn't like the creamed liver and potato meals, but she sure was fond of the peanut butter and tomato soups which she announced to Samantha every time after they were served.

"Did you eat the apple, too, this time?" Samantha asked, one eyebrow raised.

"Half. I traded Billy Lorenzo for half of his cookie," Talia added sagely. "I had to really talk him into it, though."

"I bet you did." Samantha smirked as they approached the school. She bent down to hug her daughter, noticing for the first time a run in her tights. "When did this happen?" she asked in dismay.

"I don't know. Maybe from the slide?"

"I guess I'll just have to buy you a new pair. Now, off you go."

"Bye, Mommy!" Talia raced into the school's main entrance at a full sprint, her leather-bound books bouncing behind her.

Samantha watched as her daughter disappeared, feeling the usual emotions of pride and worry in equal measure, just like every other mother on the sidewalk waving goodbye to their kids.

. . .

THE USUAL HIVE of activity and corresponding noises in the pit abruptly diminished as Samantha made her way to her desk. She kept her eyes forward, attuned to the annoyed scowls directed her way. She settled into her desk chair, her eyes glued to a copy of the morning edition placed there. Of course, she'd seen it this morning, having read it already a thousand times.

Above the photos of Cyril and Thelma Sikes and the news of their win, the headline read: SUSPECTED MURDER AT DANCE MARATHON.

She'd quoted the piece over the telephone from the marathon the night before, and she noted it was printed almost word for word. It accompanied an older photograph of Regis North and Bernice Prescott, dancing, shortly after Mr. Baines had been disqualified.

Samantha gave Johnny Milwaukee a sideways glance. He sat at his desk, leaning way back with his feet up, his fingers gripping a cigarette. Absent was his usual roguish grin. Instead, he considered her with narrowed eyes and tight lips.

He'd been scooped by her and was none too pleased.

"She died of exhaustion like all of 'em do,"

Freddy Hall snapped. "This 'murder' angle is just a ploy to get an undeserved byline."

Johnny puffed on his cigarette as he shook his head. "Nah, it's probably true. Miss Hawke here is close with the medical examiner. She was there last night and called the cops. By the time I'd clued in, she'd already called Archie."

Samantha lifted a shoulder, casting a dismissive, unapologetic shrug. It might've been a slightly underhanded thing for her to do, but there wasn't a single man in the room who wouldn't have done the same to her in a heartbeat.

And she had Talia to think about. Every byline was a boost to her career and her pocketbook.

"Miss Hawke!"

It seemed to Samantha that the entire room turned their heads at once toward the sound of Archie August shouting from his office. She planned to give him a megaphone for Christmas.

Ignoring the burning glare of all the men, especially the heat coming from Johnny, and Freddy Hall, she crossed the pit and entered Mr. August's smoke-filled office. The editor motioned for her to step up to the opposite end of the desk, where he pushed over the morning edition.

He took his cigar out of his mouth and jabbed it

in the air at her, "You made the right decision phoning this in last night. No one else has got this in time for this morning's edition, only a piece on the winners. It's a bona fide scoop!"

"Thank you, sir."

"Milwaukee is none too happy about it, of course, since he has been covering the marathon longer than you," Mr. August said. He jabbed the photograph of the winners with a stubby finger. "Why you didn't snap any of the body on the floor?" Mr. August said. "That would have been even more sensational. Were you too emotional or somethin'?"

"What? No. I—"

"Hey, you're a woman."

Samantha frowned. "Thanks for noticing."

"No, I mean . . . you know? Women can't always handle that kind of stuff. Dead bodies and things. It's understandable." He spread his hands out before him, some cigar ash falling to his lap as he did so. He roughly brushed it to the floor.

Clearly, he'd forgotten about Dr. Haley Higgins, Chief Medical Examiner. Samantha was tempted to throw that in her boss's face but bit her tongue instead.

"Actually, I got a few photographs."

Archie August stared at her blankly for a second,

then put up his hand as if to silence her. He then got up from his chair, walked past her, and softly shut the door.

"Okay, what are you playing at?" He sat back down with a grunt. "Those pictures should have been under this headline. We could have had them developed overnight here."

"Dr. Higgins, the medical examiner on the scene, made me promise to share the photographs with her before they were published. I agreed in exchange for the story."

"Well, make sure they get developed this morning. Maybe we can get them for a follow-up story this evening, even though the other papers were there last night and might have gotten a few shots." Mr. August sighed, leaned back in his chair, and motioned he was done with her for now.

"I'll get on that right away, sir."

Johnny was sitting on the edge of her desk, waiting for her when she returned. "I guess congrats are in order, doll." His face was uncharacteristically deadpan.

"Better late than never," she returned. She tapped his foot that blocked her chair. "If you don't mind, I have work to do."

Johnny shifted to his feet. "Sure thing, doll." He

sauntered away as if he hadn't a care in the world. And he probably didn't . . . and didn't want to, which was why Samantha had to keep her complicated life to herself. Even if she had room for romance, Johnny Milwaukee was not the right guy.

She risked a glance and found Johnny staring at her again. He grinned crookedly, his eyes glinting with amusement.

Nope. Definitely not.

9

*H*aley removed the stomach from the corpse of Bernice Prescott, poured the contents into a flask, then returned the organ to the abdominal cavity. Dr. Martin had done a fine job of sawing through the rib cage, which hung open like a set of morbid curtains.

Dr. Martin took notes as Haley quoted. "Stomach contents are watery; the last meal was apparently bread and pea soup."

"Very much like Mr. Baines."

"Yes, but interestingly no evidence of carrots being consumed by either."

"Which makes the carrot essence initially detected even more curious."

"Agreed. Dr. Martin, I fear they are both the

victims of foul play and quite likely by the same person."

"Any guesses what poison killed her?" Dr. Martin asked.

"Something that could be dissolved in water," Haley said. "I could guess, but I won't. Let's wait for the laboratory reports to come back." The telephone rang as Haley soaped up her hands. She shared a look with her assistant, and he jumped to answer.

"Boston City Morgue."

Covering the receiver with one hand, he announced, "It's Dr. Mitchell for you."

Lifting a slimy hand to show that she was otherwise engaged, she said, "Tell him I'll call him back."

"Dr. Mitchell, Dr. Higgins is just finishing up an autopsy. She'll be happy to call you back later."

"What did he say?" Haley asked as Dr. Martin picked up his clipboard and returned to her. "Only that he's sorry he missed you again."

Again.

It couldn't be helped. Haley was hardly responsible for the timing and frequency of Boston's dead. Her job had its demands, and as a fellow practitioner, Gerald understood that. Besides, hadn't Haley demonstrated incredible patience and understanding these last many years as Gerald held her at arm's length while he tended to his nearly comatose and incapacitated wife?

She'd passed away recently, releasing Gerald to pursue Haley more intentionally, and at first, Haley thought she'd be glad of it.

Now, she wasn't quite sure. She had enjoyed their easygoing friendship that had no strings and no expectations. The playing field had changed with Gerald's new marital status, and Haley hadn't found her footing.

"... you could meet Mitzie."

Haley's attention snapped back to the moment, and she realized Dr. Martin had been speaking.

"I'm sorry, my mind drifted. "Who's Mitzie?"

"My new girl."

"Oh?" The string of girls on Dr. Martin's arm of late was hard to keep track of.

"She's eager to meet you, and I thought, maybe if it's not too presumptuous for me to ask, we could double date with you and Dr. Mitchell."

"Double date?" Haley squirmed. She hadn't even thought of herself and Gerald officially dating in the single style. "I don't think I'm up to that, Dr. Martin, but I'd be happy to meet her if you'd like to show her the morgue sometime."

Dr. Martin's eyes lost their sparkle of enthusiasm, but he quickly recovered. "Of course. It was silly of me to ask."

Having found her rhythm stitching up the Y incision, Haley was about to ask Dr. Martin to take the samples to the laboratory when the idea turned her thoughts to the new head of the Massachusetts General Hospital Laboratory, Dr. Ronan Murphy. Without thinking about the primary reasons, Haley decided to take the samples to the lab herself.

Haley untied her bloodstained apron. "Dr. Martin, would you be so kind as to finish up for me?"

She was at the sink, washing her hands, knowing her assistant's answer.

"Of course, Doctor. If someone calls, where should I say you've gone?"

"I'm just taking the samples to the lab."

Haley didn't miss his look. Why suddenly was she doing a chore she usually sent him on? A glint in his eyes caused her enough alarm that he might guess her ulterior motives that she made a quick excuse, keeping her gaze averted. "I need to use the ladies."

Dr. Martin smirked. "I should tell a caller you've gone to the ladies?"

"No, I– Never mind. I'll be back shortly. For crying out loud, Dr. Martin. Just take a message."

In her eagerness to get out of Dr. Martin's

curious gaze, she nearly forgot to take the tray of samples with her. She spun on the heels of her low slip-on shoes, carefully collected the tray, and with head held high, pushed open the morgue doors into the hallway.

She shook her head, mentally chastising herself. She was no better than any of the silly, man-crazy nurses in the hospital, giggling and gossiping about the handsome new doctor.

She wasn't like that. She had a head on her shoulders and was too busy for romance. Anyone could ask Gerald about that.

Poor Gerald. She'd been neglecting him of late.

With a fortifying breath and new determination to remain professional, she headed up one flight of stairs to the hospital laboratory.

As serendipity would have it, Dr. Murphy was at the main desk, the young receptionist trying hard not to ogle at him but failing.

"Hello, Dr. Murphy," Haley said with a steady voice.

"Hello, Dr. Higgins."

Haley caught her breath. There was a reason the female population of the hospital was all agog. Dr. Murphy had a chiseled face with a slight sprinkling of freckles, crystal-clear blue eyes, and sultry hooded eyelids. Auburn hair with Irish red highlights was combed over to one side and shaved close to the face at the temples.

Haley and Ronan Murphy had been introduced, naturally, yet Haley's knees melted at the sound of the warm brogue that reminded her of her own heritage.

His smile deepened. "How can I help you?"

Haley refused to flirt and got straight to the point. "These samples come from the body of Bernice Prescott—"

"The marathon dancer?"

Haley nodded. "I believe she and her former partner, Patrick Baines, may have been poisoned. Are you still working on Mr. Baines' tests?"

"We are nearly finished. Tested for alcohol, illicit drugs, all the most common culprits, and so far, nothing of note."

"Maybe with these samples, you can go directly to testing for the more unusual poisons. I suspect both victims were killed the same way."

Taking the sample tray from Haley, he held her gaze. No taller than her, he was at least five years younger and ten times prettier. Except in her wildest dreams, they'd never be a match, and Haley was nothing if not a realist.

She almost pushed a curl behind her ear but caught herself in time. Remaining serious, she thanked the gorgeous doctor and turned away, rather proud of herself for being the only single woman in the hospital not throwing herself at the man.

She was still congratulating herself on her emotional feat when she returned to the morgue.

Dr. Martin, who was just drying his hands on a towel, tossed her a grin. "How's Dr. Manly?"

"Dr. Martin!" Haley was appalled at her assistant's insightfulness. She recovered by exhorting, "Please exhibit professional courtesy."

"So sorry, Doctor," Dr. Martin said, his face losing its smile. "It's just all the females in the hospital seem to have lost their senses. I should've known better than to group you in with those. Say, let me make it up to you by buying lunch."

Haley accepted his apology, though she hardly deserved it. "A Reuben for me, thank you."

Returning to her desk, Haley picked up the telephone and called Gerald. His voice would bring her down to earth and back to reality. The ringing on the other end went unanswered, and Haley sighed as she hung the receiver back on its cradle. "We're like ships in the night."

Samantha's entry followed a knock on the morgue door.

"Haley, it's just me."

"Come on in," Haley said, motioning to her friend through the glass wall.

Samantha joined her, taking the chair opposite Haley's desk. "You must've seen the headlines today."

Haley pushed her folded paper toward Sam. "I did. Congratulations on the byline."

"Thank you. The guys in the pit all have their undies in a knot."

Haley shot Samantha a perplexed look. "Why?"

"I didn't tell Johnny that Miss Prescott's death was a suspected murder and called it in to Mr. August myself. Big crime. Lady reporter bypasses the men to do her job."

Haley laughed. "That should be the next news headline. But he got the piece on the Sikeses, winning a dance marathon again. That's news."

Samantha stabbed the paper with a long fingernail. "Mr. August put that story on the fold. Like I said, the guys aren't happy with me."

"Those poor men," Haley offered facetiously. Her eyes went to the manila envelope under Samantha's arm. "Are those the photographs?"

"Uh-huh. I've had a good look at them and can't see anything that points to the murderer. Mr. August wasn't too pleased. 'Nothin' here I can print without being taken to the cleaners for printing graphic material.' I must be getting desensitized. To me, it's just a dead girl with a funny look on her face."

Haley took the envelope then emptied its contents onto her desk. A quick tug on the chain of the green-shaded banker's lamp added extra light. The images were dark from lack of proper lighting. Miss Prescott's body lay on the floor in such a way that one could be forgiven for assuming that she was simply sleeping. Except for the circles around her eyes, which all the dancers had, as the death hadn't resulted from physical trauma, there were no visible abrasions or contusions.

"Am I right?" Samantha asked. "Nothing of note?"

"It seems that way." Haley pushed stubborn loose curls off her face. "It's always nice if a killer leaves an obvious clue, but that's not usually the case."

Samantha dug in her handbag and produced her notebook and pencil. "If you're interested: my list of suspects."

Haley leaned back in her chair. "Shoot."

"Obviously, Cyril and Thelma Sikes. They were the favorites to win, so Regis and Miss Prescott, the bet to come in second, were real threats."

"Not to mention that they were upset that Mr. North and Miss Prescott hadn't been disqualified," Haley added.

"Exactly. Then there's Mr. Farber, the organizer."

Haley inclined her head. "Why would he kill Miss Prescott?"

"I don't know. But he had access to both victims."

Haley agreed that Mr. Farber deserved a deeper look.

"After that," Samantha sighed, "I have to include Regis and Gladys."

"Aren't you good friends?"

"Gladys and I were when we were younger. We drifted apart over the years but ran into each other a while back. We've had coffee together a few times."

Haley thought about those who were closest physically to Miss Prescott. The other dancers on the floor would have had little time or energy to pull off a poisoning, though she and Samantha had made allowances for the Sikeses despite this. Perhaps because they were experienced on the dance circuit, and both seemed driven enough to do whatever was deemed necessary to win.

There were also the nurses on the floor who attended the dancers during their breaks.

"Nurse Winkley," Haley said.

"Huh?"

"She tended to Miss Prescott on her last break before her collapse. I witnessed it. She needs to be on the list."

Samantha scratched at her notepad. "I wonder if she was the nurse who tended to Mr. Baines before he collapsed as well."

Haley held Samantha's gaze. "I suppose someone should ask her."

Dr. Martin returned with a paper bag containing their lunch. Haley took her Reuben and turned to Samantha. "I'll share."

Outside, as they nibbled on their sandwiches, Haley suggested they divide and conquer. "It saves time and energy."

"Okay," Samantha said. "I'll go see Gladys."

"And I'd like to have a word with Nurse Winkley."

10

*R*egis and Gladys North lived just a short walk from North Station in a brick, four-story, walk-up tenement building in Boston's west end. It was a part of town where immigrants from diverse backgrounds—from Syrians to Eastern Europeans to Irish, a large contingent of black Americans, and blue-collar workers who still had jobs—were crowded into tight apartments too small for families.

Samantha watched a group of young kids as they played stickball on the street.

The narrow building, only three windows wide, was one of the dozens crammed into the area. The distinguishing feature on this one was a huge full-color billboard taking up three of the four stories, advertising Wrigley's brand spearmint gum.

The stairs creaked like an old man's back as Samantha made her way up to where the Norths lived on the top floor. The walls were scuffed and chipped, and a faint smell of mold lingered in the air.

Samantha knocked, and Regis North opened the door, looking tired and washed-out. Though he had bathed and put on fresh clothes, dark bags hung under his eyes, and his shoulders sloped with fatigue as he regarded her standing in the dimly lit hallway.

"I hope it's all right," Samantha said apologetically. "Gladys said I could stop by."

Gladys's voice reached from inside the apartment, sounding just as tired. "Is that Sam?"

"Ya sure, c'mon in," Regis said as he stepped aside. "We just woke up—slept for a solid fifteen hours!"

The place had seen better days. The top-floor apartment had a large balcony overlooking an empty lot, and though it was clean and tidy, the furnishings were mismatched and worn, the accessories sparse. It had the feel of transition, a place a person stayed at instead of lived.

A moment later, Gladys appeared from the bedroom dressed in a natty housecoat.

"Hi, Sam." Gladys raised her hands slightly and then let them drop to her sides. "Well, as you can see, we survived." She glanced at Regis, who gave a stiff nod.

"I think it'll take a few days at least to start feeling normal," he returned with a meaningful gaze at his wife. "That baby needs some rest now."

"I am sure it's fine, Regis." Gladys gestured for Samantha to sit on the sofa before sitting down on one of the kitchen chairs. Regis collapsed on a rather well-worn upholstered lounge chair.

"Thanks for meeting with me," Samantha said. "Have you seen the headline?

"Yes, we did," Gladys nodded. "Read it over breakfast. Congratulations on the byline! I bet the boys in the pen aren't happy they got scooped by a woman."

"They're not," Samantha admitted, "but my boss, Mr. August, sure is. He sent me out right away to get some reactions from the dancers, which is why I'm here. There's going to be a follow-up story."

Gladys and Regis shared a look of apprehension. Then Gladys said, "I haven't offered you coffee or tea yet." As she rose from her seat, Samantha raised a palm, stopping her.

"It's all right, Gladys. I've already had two coffees this morning."

An awkward quiet descended as Samantha poised her pencil over her notebook.

"I . . . I know this seems strange, seeing us living like this," Gladys said, looking at her hands.

Samantha stared back quizzically. "What do you mean?"

Gladys waved a hand, indicating her humble abode. "Well, this. We'd always lived in nice places until Regis and his investments."

Regis jumped to his feet. "I'm not doing this again, Gladys." With a stiff gait, he stormed out to the balcony.

Out the window, Samantha saw a small winter garden planted in boxes, all gone to seed.

"You'll have to forgive him, Sam," Gladys said. "I shouldn't have brought it up in front of him. It's just . . . I have this compulsion to explain to people how this happened."

"Many people lost money in the crash," Samantha said gently.

"Yes, but we trusted certain people . . . we were lied to. You'd be surprised who sports a forked tongue."

"I'm sorry," Samantha said. Her fortunes had

gone the other way. After spending many years in the tenements, she now lived in a ritzy apartment on the other side of town and had money put away for Talia's future, thanks to Talia's no-good dad and his nefarious ways. Samantha would spin that story for Talia when the time came.

Regis's motion outside caught their attention as he picked through the garden, plucked weeds, and tossed them into a pail. "He wants to move back to Maine," Gladys said. "His family has a farm." Her hand settled on her stomach. "He wants to raise the baby there."

"And you don't want to?" Samantha asked.

"I'm a city girl, Sam, like you. I need the hustle and bustle around me. Farm life is too quiet, and a lot of hard work. But—" she paused, exhaling. "We could have a decent garden. Besides dancing, growing things is something Regis and I both like to do. Our garden's not big, but you'd be surprised at what we can grow."

"Couldn't he go back to work as a gardener?" Samantha asked.

Gladys laughed out loud. "In Boston, in the winter? With this depression, no one's in the market for a gardener, not even city parks."

"His education in botany must mean something," Samantha said.

"Turns out that interest in botany is a hobby, not a job, and like I said, we got bills."

Samantha cast a glance at her notes, needing to turn the conversation back to her job. "I want to talk about your thoughts on the end of the marathon if you don't mind."

"I don't mind." Gladys cast a glance at the balcony, catching Regis's eye. His shoulders slumped in a noticeable sigh, and he came back inside.

"Hey, Samantha, do you need carrots or turnips? There are still a few roots in the garden."

Samantha smiled at Regis's attempt to smooth things over. "Thank you, but I'm fine for now."

Regis ran a hand through his mussed hair and dropped into a chair, slouching, with long legs bent out in front of him. "What do you want to know?"

"Well, our readers would like to know how you felt about losing to the Sikeses," Samantha said, adding quickly, "I'm sorry, I know it's a sensitive subject."

Gladys's expression grew cold. "They're cheaters. Always have been."

Samantha couldn't hold in her surprise. "What makes you say that?"

Glancing away, Gladys mumbled. "It's just a feeling. I shouldn't have said anything."

Samantha couldn't let that go. "Do you think Cyril and Thelma Sikes would stoop to murder to win?"

"Somebody did," Regis said. "Right? You printed it yourself."

"Yes," Samantha admitted, "but it's an allegation, and no one was named. Why do you think it was the Sikeses?"

"Besides the obvious?" Regis's knee jumped wildly. "Bernice was doing well. She was tired, yes, but it seems strange to me that she collapsed so suddenly."

Gladys interrupted. "The medical examiner . . . what was her name again?"

"Dr. Haley Higgins," Samantha answered.

"Yes, Dr. Higgins. Does she really think it was murder? How sure is she about that?"

"I can't say. The postmortem is underway, and she's awaiting laboratory results. She has released no information to the press yet."

As if she was not quite satisfied with that answer, Gladys's eyes narrowed. "But how was she murdered?"

Regis answered for Samantha. "Everyone is

going to guess a poison, Gladys. I mean, she wasn't shot, and I certainly didn't strangle her so . . ."

Gladys glared at her husband. "Don't be so dramatic!"

"But I was stunned when she dropped," Regis continued. "I mean, just minutes before she was wincing in pain, but we were all in pain, and then, *bam*! Down she went. Halfway through the derby race, she was egging me on instead of the other way around."

Samantha scratched notes in her notepad, then brought the discussion back to the dance competitors. "Going into this, were you dismayed that the Sikeses, the obvious favorites, had also entered?"

"We really thought we could've beaten those guys," Regis said confidently. "I'm in good shape, and so is Gladys. We've been training hard, what with going up and down these stairs every day for a couple of years now. We even trained ourselves to go on less sleep." He glanced at Samantha sheepishly. "This was before we knew a baby was coming."

"We competed in the last marathon that the Sikeses won," Gladys said. "We almost beat them, except . . ."

There was another shared glance between the

married couple before Regis said, "I rolled my ankle. A dumb, dumb mistake."

"It's all right, honey," Gladys said gently. "We'll win the next one." She patted her growing stomach. "After the baby."

"Any idea who might have had a motive to kill Bernice Prescott?" Samantha asked.

"I think it's quite clear to me," Gladys said, raising an eyebrow. "the Sikeses. This is the fourth marathon they have entered and won. They've become famous in the whole eastern United States and have won a lot of money. They knew Bernice and Patrick were strong contenders, having won the marathon three months ago in Rochester."

"So, you think the Sikeses killed both Bernice Prescott and Patrick Baines?" Regis asked.

Samantha paused her writing and looked at both Regis and Gladys. "I wasn't aware that Patrick Baines' death has been ruled as a murder."

"Well, not yet," Regis returned stiffly.

"It only makes sense," Gladys offered. "I mean, it wouldn't surprise me."

Samantha would have to press Haley more on that point.

Gladys wasn't finished. "Not only that, I think they take something to help them win."

Samantha looked up from her notes. "Take something? Like what? Cocaine?"

Cocaine had been outlawed in 1920, but unfortunately, the market for the enhancement drug was well established. Judicial use could aid a person's endurance capability in a situation like marathon dancing.

Gladys looked back smugly. "Cheaters cheat."

Samantha had to wonder, was Gladys onto something?

11

*D*r. Martin produced an address for Nurse Winkley, a residential building for nurses only a block away from the hospital. After handing Samantha the keys to her 1928 DeSoto, Haley strolled down the street, her mind on Mr. Baines and Miss Prescott. Who had administered the poison that had brought on their deaths, and how was it done without notice?

The early spring breeze blew cold off the Charles River, and Haley tightened the belt of her wool coat, thankful that its length protected her legs and the fur collar warmed her neck. Her hat, sitting small and to the side of her head, did little to shield her ears—not even doing its job to conceal the strands of gray. Haley wondered why she bothered with hats at all. She had accepted another social conformity, fashion trends changing and disrupting lives much like this blasted spring wind.

Nurses in black capes and starched white headdresses passed Haley on the sidewalk, nodding in acknowledgment, and in one instance, greeting Haley by name.

"Hello, Dr. Higgins."

Haley was known more by reputation than appearance since most of her work was done with the dead rather than the living. She asked about Nurse Winkley.

"Oh Mildred, poor thing," the nurse returned. "She got the short straw and had to work the marathon. We're all so glad that dreadful thing is over."

"Is she in?" Haley asked.

The nurse nodded. "I think she's going to sleep for a week after that experience."

Haley thanked the nurse and continued into the lobby of the nurses' residence. A directory attached names to apartment numbers, and Haley found M. Winkley next to 220. Taking the wooden staircase to the second floor, she found her door and knocked.

A raspy voice reached her. "Go away."

"Nurse Winkley? It's Dr. Higgins."

"Oh. Just a minute."

Haley heard shuffling on the other side of the door and imagined the nurse scrambling to tidy up. When the door opened, Haley immediately apologized.

"I'm so sorry for dropping in unannounced."

"Dang it." The nurse's hand went to her lopsided curls. "I'm not showered, and I've been so busy with work, well, the place is a mess."

"I promise not to look too closely," Haley said. "May I come in?"

Nurse Winkley waved her inside. The apartment was very small, only a bedroom, bath, and joined kitchen and living area with mismatched furnishings. It smelled of stew, likely coming from the scorched pot sitting on the gas stove. A side table worked as a room divider, and Haley stopped to view a framed photograph of a rather large family.

"Those are my parents and my siblings. The youngest one there in the front," she said with fondness, "is my little brother Billy."

"Attractive bunch," Haley said, then claimed the nearest chair.

"Do ya want a drink or something? I have a Coca-Cola in the cupboard. Or if you're hungry, there's stew."

"I'm fine. I won't be long." Haley straightened her skirt. "You were one of the medical personnel tending Miss Prescott and Mr. Baines. I have a few questions."

Nurse Winkley slowly lowered herself onto the couch, pushing unfolded laundry out of the way. "Yes, well, it's always very upsetting when someone dies. Even as a nurse, I never get used to it. Sometimes I wonder if I'm in the right profession."

"Nursing can be very trying," Haley acknowledged. "I nursed during the war in France and England."

The younger woman's eyes filled with a glint of admiration. "I've never been to Europe. Should've gone in the twenties when there was more money to burn, but I was in nursing school then, and well, other things were going on, and now—" She rubbed her forefinger and thumb together, indicating a lack of funds.

"It's a tough time for many," Haley said, "which is why brutish events like these dance marathons are a success. Anyway, back to our dead—I saw you tend to Bernice Prescott in the break before the derby. What was it that you did for her, exactly?"

Nurse Winkley frowned, and Haley realized her question sounded close to an accusation. She quickly amended it by adding, "I'm looking for any clue you might've noticed."

"I see, well . . ." Nurse Winkley's gaze cast upward. "The dancers always collapse on their cots, no matter how hungry or thirsty they are or if they have to use the restrooms. Each nurse tends to two or three dancers. I always offered water first, then roused them to take a bathroom break. But—"

"Yes?"

"Well, Miss Prescott said she didn't have to go. I immediately suspected she was dehydrated, so I gave her extra water."

"Where did you get the water from?"

"There were several pitchers on the table. The catering staff kept them filled. I poured her a glass."

Nurse Winkley would have had the opportunity to drop something into a glass before giving it to Miss Prescott. Haley remembered seeing the nurse and the dancer together, but there were plenty of other people around as well. All the other dancers, the officials, the nurses, and family members were allowed into the recovery section for moral and emotional support, including Gladys North, who, Haley now recalled, was by her husband's side.

"Did you attend Mr. Baines the night he died?" Haley asked.

"Well, yes, but only because his regular nurse had her hands full with Mrs. Sikes." Nurse Winkley sniffed. "That woman can be a handful. She thinks because she's won a marathon before she's the Queen of Sheba."

"So, you weren't supposed to tend to Mr. Baines?"

"No, but we all just do what we have to."

"Did you notice anything strange about Mr. Baines's behavior or condition before his collapse?"

Nurse Winkley wrinkled her nose. "Dancers at that stage of the game all smell bad, look like death, and are barely coherent. I pitied him because I could tell he would not make it to the end."

"How so?"

"His skin was grayish and his breath—"

"Smelled like carrots?"

Nurse Winkley's gaze shifted upward as though she was thinking back. "You know, now that you mentioned it, yeah, it did. So did Miss Prescott's. Like overcooked carrots."

"Did you know either Mr. Baines or Miss Prescott before the marathon began?"

Nurse Winkley stiffened; her gaze suddenly looked guarded. "Not really. I mean, Bernice lived in the same neighborhood as I did when I grew up, but we didn't hang out together." She raised a finger. "But, if you're looking for a bad guy, talk to Mr. Farber. I've never met anyone so ruthless. He'd sell his mother for a dollar."

Haley had every intention of speaking with the dance organizer.

"He came across as such to me as well," Haley said. "Did you witness anything? Did Mr. Farber, Mr. Baines, or Miss Prescott have words?"

"Not exactly. He barked at everyone equally. I just don't like him."

Haley hadn't warmed to the man, either, but being obnoxious wasn't a crime in America and not proof that one was predisposed to committing murder.

12

*S*amantha made a telephone call from the pit, which finally yielded an interview appointment with Cyril and Thelma Sikes. Apparently, every newspaper in Boston was trying to get a journalist in front of the celebrity couple for a few minutes. They lived south of Boston Common, a nicer neighborhood than the Norths, but with a similar red-brick design.

Cyril Sikes opened the door, and Samantha was hit with the familiar aroma of bologna casserole, a meal that she herself had cooked many times in the last few years.

"Welcome, Miss Hawke," Mr. Sikes said with a smile. He led Samantha to the open kitchen which was large, warm, and more like Haley's than Gladys

North's, with modern appliances, and south-facing windows brightening the room with daylight.

Thelma Sikes turned from the stovetop. "Hi, Miss Hawke."

Like the Norths, the Sikeses looked bone-tired, but hunger demanded expenditure of energy. Mrs. Sikes gestured to an empty kitchen chair. "Have a seat."

Samantha accepted. "Thank you. It smells terrific in here."

"Ah, you're too kind. It's only bologna casserole."

She held a large kitchen knife in one hand, which she waved lazily in the air, and in the other, a large parsnip, scrubbed clean. "Frying these on the side. Hard to come by a proper vegetable these days."

"The farmers will plant again soon," Mr. Sikes said. He took a chair opposite Samantha, let his knees fall open, and lit a cigarette. "Not that I get excited over rabbit food."

"Thanks for meeting with me," Samantha said. "I know you have had reporters hounding you. After what you've been through, you must be exhausted."

"No trouble at all," Mrs. Sikes said. "You're the second reporter to come by, but I was particularly eager to meet you." As she lowered herself into a chair, Sam noticed a certain wildness in Mrs. Sikes's eyes. "A woman reporter! Good for you. Your family must be proud. Are you married? How does your husband feel about it? What about your kids? Oh my goodness, they must be over the moon."

The sudden barrage of questions caused Samantha to blink in quick succession.

"I . . . um."

"C'mon, Thelma," Mr. Sikes said, coming to the rescue. "She's the one supposed to be asking questions here."

"I'm a widow, and I have one daughter." Samantha smiled. "Yes, she is proud of me."

"Wonderful!" Mrs. Sikes said. "Well, I don't mean your husband dying, but about your daughter being proud." She returned to the stove where the parsnips were frying.

"So, Miss Hawke, shoot." Mr. Sikes leaned back on his chair and ran his fingers through his hair which was in need of a trim.

"Okay then. Let's start with your history. The two of you have already won three marathons in—" Samantha scanned her notes. "Two in New York and one in Philadelphia. Is that right?"

"Yes!" Mrs. Sikes said suddenly, but she looked into her frying pan as both Samantha and Mr. Sikes stared at her. It wasn't clear if she was answering the question or was just excited that the parsnips were now browned. She dumped the contents of the cutting board into the frying pan and then, without looking at either of them, reached over, turned on the sink faucet, and scrubbed her hands with a bar of soap. Samantha considered Mrs. Sikes's strange, frenetic energy, and Gladys's accusation came to mind. Mrs. Sikes was acting like someone under the influence of cocaine.

"That's right," Mr. Sikes replied calmly. "This was our fourth straight victory. We started with a smaller marathon out in Worcester. That was our introduction to this whole thing. We came in second and won $250. That took us out of the worst hole. It convinced us we could win big money if we tried harder, right Thelma?"

"A new way to make a living. That's what I told you back then, Cyril. You remember?"

"Of course I do, dear. You were right too. Look at us now."

"It's very impressive," Samantha admitted. Winning a dance marathon wasn't an easy way to make a living, but the cash prize was life changing, and the celebrity status that came with it brought along other perks. "What did you do for a living before?"

Mr. Sikes let go of a plume of smoke that joined the haze snuggling the yellowing ceiling.

"Pharmacist. Good job until the panic. Got let go last year. Few people can afford that kind of thing right now."

"You're a trained pharmacist?" Samantha couldn't hold in her surprise. Mr. Sikes, in his sleeveless shirt and mussed up hair, didn't have the look of a professional. The countrywide depression had taken its toll quickly.

Mr. Sikes grinned smugly. "Class of twenty-seven, Massachusetts College of Pharmacy."

"He was the top of his class," Mrs. Sikes said as she opened a can of pork and beans. "We got married later that year. Cyril looked so handsome on our wedding day. Everyone said so, even my ma, God rest her soul, and she was never one for flattery, let me tell you. Neither was my pa. He passed away ten years ago from tuberculosis. Terrible disease. I remember . . ."

"Thelma." Cyril cocked his head and raised an eyebrow.

"Right, stay on subject." Mrs. Sikes's face went blank, and she stood for a moment without moving. "I'm going to lie down," she said suddenly and walked out of the kitchen without looking at

Samantha or her husband.

Cyril shouted after her, "Wait, what about the casserole?"

"Can you see to it? Just take it out of the oven in five minutes."

"Don't mind her," Cyril said after the sound of a closing door. He dropped a long lump of ash into the ashtray. "She doesn't like to admit it, but these marathons take a lot out of her. Out of both of us."

"Mr. Sikes, what do you know about people using certain . . . um . . . substances to help them win contests like this?"

His jaw twitched. "You mean like narcotics?"

"Yes, there have been incidences where people have used things like cocaine to help them win."

"That would be illegal," he said as he stepped toward the oven.

"Yes, it would."

Mr. Sikes turned, locking his gaze on Samantha. "I hope you're not trying to paint us with that brush for your paper, Miss Hawke." He used a tea towel to remove the hot casserole and set it on top of the stove. "I see how it would be a sensational story, but I'm afraid we'll have to disappoint you on that front."

"Of course." Samantha smiled, hoping to relieve Mr. Sikes's concerns. She wasn't ready for the interview to end and didn't want to give the man a reason to throw her out. "Tell me, what would you say is the secret to your successes?"

"It's not as spectacular as illegal substances." Mr. Sikes returned to his seat and lit up another cigarette, either nervous by Samantha's questions or a chain smoker. Possibly both.

"We win because we're in top shape and have strong constitutions. We have grit, you might say."

"Some people would say that might make for a stormy marriage; two strong-willed people." Samantha, always the journalist, probed for a new angle on the story.

"Maybe, but it is also the secret of our successes." Mr. Sikes nodded toward her notepad. "Now I don't want to read in your article that I said we have a stormy marriage. I didn't say that."

"Of course not."

Satisfied, Mr. Sikes continued, seemingly eager to set the record straight. "Once we made our first thousand dollars, there was no looking back, especially when the advertising endorsements started to come in. We moved into this apartment and were determined to keep going. I have a new Plymouth parked out there on the street." He nodded toward the front of the building. "Like I said, Miss Hawke, a person needs grit to be successful in these trying times. Grit and determination. Nothing else will motivate a winner."

Samantha guessed it was the same little inspirational speech he had given to the other reporters. She decided on another tack.

"Speaking of motives, what do you make of this whole suspected murder thing?"

"Yeah, I read your byline, Miss Hawke. Tabloid news, I say. A little beneath you, isn't it?" Mr. Sikes leaned forward, bracing his elbows on his knees. "Maybe your doctor friend made a mistake. No reason that Bernice didn't die of exhaustion, plain and simple."

"Did you know that Miss Prescott and Patrick Baines had also won a large dance marathon in Buffalo last year? Just under two thousand hours. That's more than you and Mrs. Sikes have ever gone."

Mr. Sikes frowned. "Yes, I think I heard something about that. Dancing for nearly three months straight. Talk about grueling! Makes this last one look like it was for babies."

"Their obvious stamina didn't worry you?"

"Worried is not the right word. We knew they would be the ones to beat, yes, but we were sure we could." He smiled. "We were right." He rescued his nearly burned-to-ash cigarette from the ashtray and swore again. "Oh well," he said, stubbing it out. "Thelma says I smoke too much, anyway."

Samantha returned her notepad to her purse and pushed away from the table. "Thank you for your time, Mr. Sikes. Give my regards to Mrs. Sikes."

"Sure thing." He followed her to the door, opening it for her. "Ya know, if Bernice was bumped off, I might know something."

Samantha spun, her heart skipping a beat like it did every time she sensed important information was within her reach.

"What is it, Mr. Sikes?"

"Well, it's kind of hearsay, from Thelma. Bernice told her that the head nurse had a secret."

"Nurse Winkley?"

"Yeah, that one."

"What was the secret?"

"That's the thing, Bernice wouldn't say. I told Thelma it was nasty gossip, but I don't know, maybe it was true? Apparently, it was something shameful. Maybe that nurse took her out to keep her from talking."

13

*T*hrough a series of hits and misses, Haley tracked down Boyd Farber. He was at a dingy speakeasy by the docks. She'd been called to this establishment before in her position as Chief Medical Examiner and had made an uneasy truce with the owner. She didn't see the point in reporting him for selling liquor since it only meant the pub would spring up in another location. In exchange for her silence, he gave her entrance and information.

Mr. Farber was apparently still mid-celebration.

"Another successful venture," he roared, "though it darned near killed me."

His drinking buddy, clearly not fatigued by the subject, jibed loudly, "It killed somebody if you'd have bothered to read the headlines!" A loud guffaw followed by the surrounding fellows, who lifted a drink. "God bless her soul!"

"She ain't dead 'cuz of my dance, you nitwits," Mr. Farber shouted defensively. "Didn't you read it was murder? Not my fault, that."

Haley's entrance finally drew the attention of the small crowd, if somewhat belatedly. Mr. Farber squinted, his bushy brows forming a thick *V*. "Well, I'll be. What you doin' here, missy?"

Haley ignored the slight. "I'm looking for you, Mr. Farber."

A hoot and cheer went up as if Haley had actually propositioned the foul-smelling man. She quickly cleared up her intent. "To talk about the alleged murders that took place at your event."

"Huh? Murders?"

"Yes, there were two," Haley replied calmly. "Could we move to a quiet table to talk?"

Mr. Farber threw a bunch of coins on the counter. "See ya later, fellows. Got a serious lady who wants to talk with me."

Haley scowled at the barrage of offensive quips, happy to leave that lot of drunkards behind.

Slipping outside, Haley offered, "Can I buy you a coffee?" Before Mr. Farber could reply, she hauled him into the nearest coffee shop, claimed a booth, and ordered two cups. She waited until Mr. Farber had had a few good gulps and for his eyes to clear of intoxication before getting to the meat of the matter.

"I'm only here to ask you questions as a matter of course," she explained.

"Ain't that the cops' job?"

"Yes, well, I work with the police. Don't be surprised if a detective comes calling."

"I ain't got nothin' to hide, Doctor. I'm a businessman, on the up and up."

"As part of the dance marathon circuit, you've come into contact with the couples on occasion. Did you know Mr. Baines or Miss Prescott from before this event?"

Mr. Farber folded thick arms and leaned into the back of the booth. "Baines, huh? He's the other one that's been murdered?"

Haley nodded. "Allegedly."

"Huh. Yeah. I knew them before, but just professionally, see. Not drinking buddies. Never invited over for dinner or the like."

"What did you do before dance marathons became popular?" Haley asked. She was genuinely curious. Before the crash, most people had had occupations they now no longer worked in.

Mr. Farber sniffed. "I was an industrial chemical worker."

"Really?" Haley was sincerely surprised. His gruff entertainer, event-organizer persona must have been part of an act.

"I know, I don't come across as the educated type, and I'm not really. I didn't finish college. The war brought an end to that, but by the end of things, no one cared. I had some science courses under my belt, so that made me an expert." He gave Haley a tortured look. "I was part of a research team that made poison gas."

Mr. Farber raised a hand to the waitress, and she hurried over and refilled his coffee cup. He produced a flask from his coat pocket when she turned away and added amber liquid to his brew. "I take comfort where I can. Women can't seem to stand me, so I make love to this."

Haley kept her expression blank. Mr. Farber wasn't alone in his vice. Despite prohibition, drink—bad drink—could be found in abundance. She'd seen evidence of that in her morgue plenty of times.

"I imagine that you were privy to a lot of back-room drama during the marathon. Did you see anyone threaten either Mr. Baines or Miss Prescott?"

Mr. Farber frowned deeply as he shook his head.

"Nope. Just the normal competitive banter. *I'll get you. Watch out. You're goin' down.* That type of thing. They all said it."

Haley eyed Mr. Farber over the rim of her cup. A chemist who worked with poisonous gas could concoct a poison to take out a couple of dancers. The question was, why? What did Mr. Farber have to gain? The dance would've run its course in a couple of days, anyway. Unless he needed the Sikeses to win? Had he gambled on the couple?

She'd just have to wait for the laboratory results and hope they'd come back with something definite.

After a final sip, Haley said, "Thank you for your time, Mr. Farber."

He lifted his half-empty cup as she slipped out of the booth. "Thank you for the coffee, Doctor."

When Haley arrived at her fourth-floor apartment on Grover Street, Mrs. Berrymaple was already ensconced in her kitchen.

"Dr. Higgins," she said warmly. "I hope you don't mind, but Mrs. Rosenbaum was running late and the little one's getting hungry, and well, I thought you all might like a bite to eat. It's only mulligan stew and dumplings."

Haley couldn't deny the smell in her kitchen was

wonderful. She had smelled nothing quite like it since Molly had left to be married.

"I don't mind at all," Haley said, unpinning her hat. "It smells heavenly."

"Huh? Forgive me. I'm a little hard of hearing."

"I said it smells great!"

Mrs. Berrymaple grinned. "Glad you think so. Mrs. Rosenbaum and Talia are in their room getting ready for dinner."

Legally, Samantha's last name was Rosenbaum, as she was the widow of Seth Rosenbaum, but she went by her maiden name for work purposes. For one, it was shorter and easier to say. Still, the main reason was that, during these challenging times, women in the workforce were deeply frowned upon as it was taking jobs away from men with families to support. Short-sighted thinking as there were plenty of women, like Samantha, with families to support as well.

Samantha, with Talia in hand, entered the dining room. "I thought I heard your voice," she said to Haley. "We have a lot to catch up on."

They had an understanding—they didn't mention work until after Talia was excused from the table since it often involved talking about subjects unsuitable for her young ears.

Haley, Samantha, and Talia took their usual places, Haley and Sam on each end, with Talia on one side. Mrs. Berrymaple set the stew on a wooden cutting board in the middle of the table, then wiped her palms on her apron. "I'll be off then," she said.

Haley protested, raising her voice slightly for the older woman's benefit. "You most certainly will not! Please, you must join us. Especially after all your hard work."

Mrs. Berrymaple's eyes flashed with surprise. After a moment, she responded, "Well, all right. Let me grab another place setting."

Haley stared at the empty spot at the table and frowned. How had she missed seeing it had been set for three and not four?

When Mrs. Berrymaple had pulled her chair into position, Haley continued, "And you accept that you're always invited and included from now on."

Samantha agreed. "Yes, Mrs. Berrymaple, you are part of our family now. Talia adores you, and so do we."

Mrs. Berrymaple burst into tears.

Haley shot Samantha a worried look, then reached over to take the widow's hand.

"I'm sorry, ladies. I don't mean to cause a scene. I've just been so lonely since Edward died. I've been thinking of moving back to Canada. I have a bit of family left in New Brunswick—as you know, Edward and I never had children, not by design, I assure you —but after so many years, Boston is my home now."

Talia's young voice quivered. "Don't cry, Bubba."

When Mrs. Berrymaple flashed a confused look in Samantha's direction, Sam explained. "Bubba is what Talia called her late grandmother. It's her way of inviting you into the family."

"Now you're going to make me cry again," Mrs. Berrymaple said with a smile. "Let's eat before the stew grows cold, and I ruin it with my tears." That said, Mrs. Berrymaple took charge of the ladle and poured generous portions of stew and dumplings into each bowl.

"The dumplings are my favorite part," Talia said.

Mrs. Berrymaple gave the young girl an extra portion. "Me too, Talia. Me too."

After supper, Mrs. Berrymaple insisted on reading to Talia. "We've been reading through the *Voyages of Doctor Dolittle*, and I really need to know what happens next," she said.

Haley and Samantha settled into the living room, richly decorated with plush maroon furnishings, complementary wallpaper, and high ceilings trimmed with wood molding. A fireplace was lit, and off to the side, standing on the hardwood floor, was a large wood-crafted radio. A tall areca palm added green to the space, and the overall feel was intended for relaxation.

Breaking into her stash of illicit Canadian whiskey that she kept in a concealed cabinet behind the radio, Haley poured two small glasses.

"I feel today deserves this," she said as she handed one glass to Samantha.

On either end of the couch, they tossed off their shoes and tucked their feet underneath themselves.

"So, what have you learned since we last met up at the morgue?" Haley asked.

"Golly, that seems like eons ago."

Haley had to agree. "Some days are so full. They feel long."

"I know. I've been on my feet all day, but I don't think I've learned a darned thing. Gladys and Regis are upset they lost the dance. She's unhappy with where they live, though it's a notch or two above where I came from. Even has a balcony big enough for a small garden box. Gladys says Regis wasn't careful with their investments. Someone lied and cheated."

"That's always the story," Haley said.

"Speaking of cheating, the Norths were none too

pleased with the Sikeses, even accusing them of taking cocaine!"

Haley considered the accusation. "It's happened in athletic circles. Cocaine has stamina-feigning attributes. Did you see the Sikeses too? What did they have to say?"

"It was Mr. Sikes who did most of the talking, though Mrs. Sikes acted peculiar."

"How so?"

"Very jumpy and talkative. She was cooking and hardly stopped talking, constantly in motion. Maybe residue from having to constantly be moving all these months on the dance floor."

"I'm sure it's a big change."

"She left before I could even properly start the interview, suddenly fatigued, leaving the outcome of the bologna casserole to Mr. Sikes. He said his wife told him that Bernice Prescott knew a secret about Nurse Winkley, though he couldn't say what it was."

"Sounds like he's trying to deflect suspicion."

"Could be. Also, no one seems to know that Patrick Baines was also a victim."

"That hasn't been made public," Haley said. "Detective Cluney likes to keep some details under his hat."

"Oops." Samantha jerked, nearly spilling her

drink. "I may have given up the jig. At least with the Norths. They were surprised to hear it."

"It's bound to come out, eventually. I'm surprised that your newshounds haven't picked up on the possibility since two former dance partners are dead."

"Well, if they had, they're not going to tell me about it. Johnny's sulking."

"I thought the two of you were hitting it off," Haley said.

"We were. But his goodwill toward me only lasts when I'm working on fluff pieces and not in direct competition with him."

"I see."

"What about you and Dr. Geriatrics?"

"Old joke, Sam, and what about us? We're both so busy with work these days."

Samantha hummed. "Word on the street is there's a handsome new doctor in charge of the hospital laboratory."

Haley tucked her chin and looked up from under her eyelashes. "See, now, if you could just apply those skills to this case, we might get somewhere." Haley sipped her whiskey as Samantha laughed.

"I object to your declaration that you found out

nothing," Haley continued. "the Sikeses have means, opportunity, and motive."

"I agree," Samantha said. "We just need proof."

"Yes, however, they're not the only ones with the means and opportunity." Haley told Samantha about Nurse Winkley and Mr. Farber.

"Nurse Winkley attended both Patrick Baines and Bernice Prescott just before they fainted."

"Quite the coincidence," Samantha agreed.

"And she'd known Bernice since childhood, though she says they were never close."

"A falling out, maybe?" Samantha queried. "A final act of revenge?"

Haley lifted a shoulder. "Perhaps, but then there's Mr. Farber."

"Yes, a poison expert," Samantha said. "That's a little on the nose."

Mr. Midnight hobbled into the room, and Haley rubbed the couch cushion with one finger, getting his attention. Even with only one back leg, the feline could spring his weight onto the couch and curled up next to Haley. She stroked his soft black fur. "I know you and Gladys are friendly," she said, "but, besides bad investments, any skeletons in the closet there?"

"Gladys and Regis really wanted to win, but if

they were going to kill anyone, it would've been the Sikeses, wouldn't it?"

Haley had to concur. Their discussion was inter-rupted by Talia calling for Samantha to say her nightly prayers. Mrs. Berrymaple returned to the kitchen and started the dishes.

Haley hurried to her side. "You don't have to do that," she said.

"Oh, I don't mind. Just a quiet apartment waiting for me."

Haley grabbed a tea towel. "Then we'll do them together. Do you like to listen to the radio, Mrs. Berrymaple?"

"I do, Dr. Higgins. I believe Maxwell House Show Boat is on right about now."

14

*H*aley found solace in her home office. Her desk was tidy with a stack of science magazines to one side. A shelf was nicely filled with medical books and a collection of mystery novels, something she indulged in when she wasn't busy solving her own mysteries in real life. Her joy was the artificial putting mat that ran along the length of the room. Taking the putting iron, Haley smoothed out her trousers and putted a few balls, getting every one of them into the hole. The rather mindless activity allowed her subconscious to work, and despite what might appear obvious, Haley knew she was missing something vital.

However, after her tenth putt, nothing extraordinary had come to mind. At any rate, it was time to leave for the morgue. She put the golf club in its spot in the corner, collected the balls, dropped them into the basket they'd come from, and removed the single golfing glove she wore on her left hand.

It was as she was answering her mail that it came to her. Using the boxy, wooden wall telephone in the kitchen, she dialed the number of the morgue, thankful that Dr. Martin came to work on time.

"Dr. Martin, it's Dr. Higgins. I'm running a little late."

"Good thing it's a slow morning," he said with a chuckle. "I'll catch up on paperwork."

That settled, Haley collected her things, put on her coat and hat, and slipped on her first glove just as the two black bells on the top of the telephone rang. When Molly had lived with her, Haley would have let the housekeeper take a message. Her choice now was to leave without knowing who was on the line or pivot and pick up.

Shoot. She would wonder about the call all day and if it was important or not. It could be Samantha with news or Talia's school reporting a problem.

Her low heels clipped along the wooden floors as she hurried to the kitchen, lifted the black cylinder-shaped receiver, and held it to her ear.

"Dr. Higgins speaking."

"Haley!" Gerald's friendly voice crackled across the line. "I can't believe I finally caught you."

"Gerald! Well, you nearly didn't. I'm just on my way out the door."

"Lucky for me then."

"Yes, well, what can I do for you?"

A pause. "I'm not making a professional call, Haley. I'm wondering when you'll be free for dinner. Or lunch. Or coffee."

The muted frustrations in Gerald's tone irritated her. "I'm swamped at the moment. I've got two suspicious deaths."

"Isn't that the job of the police?"

Haley's breath caught in her throat. She and Gerald had been friends for many years, long enough for him to know how she operated with the police.

"Perhaps crime investigation isn't part of my job description, Gerald, but it's part of who I am. Apparently, Detective Cluney understands this more than you do."

"Haley, I apologize. Of course, I don't mean to impede your job or your passion. Forgive me."

Why was this man so easygoing? A part of Haley wanted to get into a rousing argument. But their friendship had never allowed for that. They were always both consistently calm and reasonable. Shouting solved nothing.

"There's nothing to forgive. I really am in a hurry, though, Gerald. I'll call you when I can. I promise."

"Of course. And if there's anything I can do to help, Haley, you know I care for you."

"Thank you, Gerald. I know."

Haley pushed back feelings of mild aggravation and hurried down the stairs. Her DeSoto was parked nearby, and when she finally settled into the driver's seat, she found she was out of breath. Gerald's voice replayed in her ear.

You know I care for you.

Suddenly, it wasn't Gerald's voice she heard in her head, but Dr. Murphy's!

Focus, Haley, she chided herself. Turning the engine, she gripped the steering wheel with gloved hands and headed toward the hospital. She needed to speak with Nurse Winkley again.

Haley knocked on Nurse Winkley's door for a third time. When the nurse failed to respond, Haley felt a pulse of concern. "Nurse Winkley?"

She tested the doorknob, and it clicked open. Even in Boston, people felt safe enough to leave their doors unlocked, at least during the day. It didn't mean the apartment was empty. Nurse Winkley could be sleeping—nurses kept strange hours—or in the shower, reasons Haley's knocking could've gone unnoticed.

Or—Haley's imagination saw Nurse Winkley on the floor. She stepped inside. "Nurse Winkley?" A quick walkthrough of the confined premises confirmed that the nurse was out.

It wasn't in Haley's nature to snoop, but she made exceptions when two murders were involved. Desperate times called for desperate measures and all that.

Haley checked the writing desk in the living room and the counters in the kitchen area, but a cursory look found nothing. She suspected if there was anything to discover, it would be in the nurse's bedroom. The bed was neatly made, and all the drawers of her dresser and night tables were closed. However, the closet door was left open, and Haley's eyes were drawn to a shoebox askew on the top shelf—out of concert with everything else that was neatly in order. Haley surmised that Nurse Winkley had removed it recently. Quite likely, the box contained shoes, but Haley's curiosity pushed her to look inside. It was times like this where she was thankful to be tall.

Even as she lifted the box, she knew it didn't contain shoes as the weight didn't correspond. Lifting the lid, Haley found personal documents and was instantly remorseful. She wouldn't like anyone snooping about in her private affairs. But she couldn't now deny what her eyes had seen.

A birth certificate for a boy, William Winkley, listing Mildred Winkley as the mother. Billy wasn't Nurse Winkley's younger brother, but her natural son, which explained why she had felt compelled to point him out in the family photograph. Unwed motherhood in 1932 was considered, by most, to be unspeakably shameful, ruining the reputation of the woman involved, and that of her whole family's. Married couples with older daughters often had "surprise babies" at a late age. No one ever talked about it when it happened, and the child often would go through their whole life not knowing their "mother" was actually their grandmother.

Most damning was a folded note, crinkled and pressed back into shape as if the recipient had crushed it into a ball in a fit of emotion. Haley could understand why: the writer was asking for money for silence. No signature, just the initials *B.P.*

Bernice Prescott?

Blackmail would be a motive for Nurse Winkley. And it would explain the scathing looks Haley had seen exchanged between the two women.

Haley returned the letter to the box and put it back into its place, ensuring its slightly crooked positioning. By all rights, she should've then left immediately, but since she was there, she needed to check for the thing that had troubled her in the first place.

That stew.

The last time she had been here, the stew was just warming on the stove. Haley had ignored the commonplace event—stew was one of the main meals for many Americans in these days, especially during the winter months. Prime cuts of meat were expensive, too expensive for most, and all most folks could hope for were leftover bones and hearty root vegetables.

The pot wasn't on the stove, but Haley thought the nurse wouldn't likely have eaten the whole pot in one sitting. She opened a pantry cupboard and found a container there. She'd only lifted the lid to take a sniff when she was startled by a demanding voice.

"What are you doing here?"

Feeling like a child caught with her hand in the cookie jar, Haley stared at Nurse Winkley.

"Nurse Winkley. I can explain."

"I'm waiting," the nurse replied, then promptly fell to the floor in a faint.

15

*H*olding a cup of coffee, Samantha closed her eyes. She sat on a bench between the imposing redbrick building of Faneuil Hall—its white, gold-capped, church-like steeple poking the sky—and Quincy Market. Sandwiched between the redbrick North Market and South Market buildings, the Greek edifice of Quincy Market stood out with its white stone and the portico entrance supported by four columns.

Samantha turned her face toward the shy, early spring sunshine and sighed deeply. The cobbled plaza was not too busy, and though the air was still crisp, she could still feel the warmth from the sun, and it felt good. She was glad she had made the last-minute decision to make her way down to Quincy Market in search of a new pair of tights for Talia.

With the new tights in a shopping bag beside her on the bench and a fresh coffee warming her hands, everything was turning out just the way she had pictured.

Except for one small thing: Johnny Milwaukee was following her.

She had spied him twice as she moved through the stalls in the market—vendors selling everything from fish to bread, vegetables to preserves. He didn't notice that she'd spotted him, but it was clear he was trying to remain unobserved. Why? Samantha hadn't any idea, but she didn't even have to turn her head to know it was him walking up behind her.

Without even opening her eyes or turning to face him, she said, "Okay, Johnny, what gives?"

"Aww, doll, how d'you know it was me?" He slouched down beside her, a Dixie cup of coffee in his hand.

"The sound of your hard-soled shoes on the cement. Most people walk. You amble."

Chuckling, he said, "I amble?" He adjusted his fedora with one hand as he sipped his coffee held in the other.

"You're either ambling or strutting," Samantha said. "I can always tell it's you walking across the pit floor without even looking."

"Is that so?" He turned to her with a raised eyebrow. "I suppose it's better than lurching like Freddie Hall." Johnny stared down at his leather shoes as if noticing them for the first time. "I'll see if I can walk more normally from now on so that I can sneak up on you better."

"Which prompts the question, why are you following me?

"I wasn't . . ."

Samantha frowned, her annoyance growing.

"Okay, I was here looking for a good chipped-beef on toast for lunch. They have them here at Squinty's Sandwich Shop."

Samantha raised her paper cup. "And yet, here you are, no sandwich."

"Yeah, well, when I saw you in the crowd, I thought it might be a good chance to talk."

"So why not just approach me to talk?"

"'Cuz you went into that dress shop. No respectable fellow would be seen inside. I had to wait it out. Then you bought your coffee, so I thought I'd do the same and join you."

Samantha wrinkled her nose at his explanation but let it ride. "Fine, whatcha wanna talk about?"

He shifted, his hand moving toward her shopping bag. She slapped his hand. "Hey, leave that alone."

"Relax, kiddo. I was just movin' it so I could put my coffee down." He lifted his cup in the air, his expression feigning hurt. "What d'ya got in there anyways?"

Samantha huffed but gave him an apologetic glance. "Boy, you're nosy today."

Johnny crossed his legs. "I'm a reporter, doll. They pay me to be nosy."

"Well, then I'll give you the big exclusive. These are new tights for Talia. Her old ones are snagged and stained, and since I'm her mom, it's up to me to earn money needed to buy them *and* to do the necessary shopping." She shook the bag at him. "Better phone it in right away. Archie August will love you for it."

"You're funny."

"It must be nice not having to worry about anyone but yourself."

Johnny stiffened. "It has its perks."

Annoyed, Samantha punched him in the arm.

"Do you even know what it's like to be concerned about someone else?"

A quick shadow crossed through Johnny's eyes as his usual cavalier expression went suddenly somber.

"We don't all wear our hearts on our sleeves, Sam."

"What do you mean by that? And don't say I'm emotional because I'm a woman."

Johnny jerked back, his eyes narrowing, and Samantha had the feeling she'd gone too far. How did this conversation get off track so quickly?

"I wouldn't dare," he finally said. "I just meant sometimes there's more to a person than what meets the surface." He turned and dumped the last few drops of his coffee onto the ground. "But that's not what I wanted to talk to you about." He lit a cigarette and took a long drag.

"Please, don't keep me in suspense."

Johnny flashed his trademark lazy smile. "I think we should work together on this whole suspected murder thing."

Samantha's feathers ruffled. "*Oh?* I didn't realize I needed help."

"Not saying you do. Just, I got stuff on the Sikeses that you don't know about."

"Like what?"

Johnny blew smoke rings into the air. "Like something that could be a motive for murder."

"You mean like the motive of the loss of substantial money and fame? I am sure you already knew that Bernice Prescott and Patrick Baines had won a marathon in Buffalo that went almost three thousand hours. That's more than the Sikeses have ever gone."

"Sure, doll, I knew that from the beginning. I'm not talking about that." His rakish grin had returned in full force.

She stared at him impatiently.

"You've got an inside track with the medical examiner," Johnny said. "I want to get in on that. If you agree to let me in on any new information from her when you get it, I will give you what I get along the way."

"To be clear, you want me to share this story with you."

"Yeah, that's it. Maybe we can even write it together. It'll be a better piece if we collaborate, don't you think?"

"I don't know, Johnny. If you want to buy in, you'd better have something good."

"Okay, doll. I see you're gonna be tough, huh? Good for you. That's exactly what I would do." He chuckled and then threw his cigarette by his feet, grinding it out with his left heel.

"How about this for a juicy tidbit?" Johnny locked his brooding eyes on Samantha. "Thelma Sikes and Patrick Baines were having an affair."

16

*H*aley followed the ambulance to the hospital, haphazardly parking her DeSoto, then ran after the gurney, her hands wrapped around the stew pot, as her purse pulsed against her side.

The door closed behind the gurney just as she reached it. Though she applied a reasonable amount of pressure on the door sufficient to open it, it flew wide beyond expectation, thrusting her into the person who'd inexplicably opened it from the other side at the same time.

She nearly knocked heads with the delectable Dr. Murphy!

"Oh, excuse me," she said breathlessly.

He held her by both arms as if she were a

fainting damsel and not the head of the pathology department. She was hardly a weak-stemmed flower. She pulled back, straightening her hat.

"Are you all right?" Dr. Murphy said.

His handsome eyes twinkled with amusement, and if she hadn't any sense at all, she would've swooned. But she was a sensible woman. "I'm fine, thank you. I'm in a hurry, though, if you don't mind."

An awkward sidestep, faux dance ensued as nurses in the hall gawked and twittered. She eyed them sternly. "Nurses, I'm sure you have work to do."

The nurses scrambled away like chastised children. Haley refused to look back at the object of their admiration but couldn't help seeing his reflection in the glassy wall of a nearby office.

Dr. Murphy was staring at her.

Haley ignored the leap her heart made and hurried toward the emergency room. She called to the nearest attendant. "I'm with the patient who was just rolled in. Nurse Mildred Winkley."

An hour later, Nurse Winkley was stabilized, though she remained unconscious. Haley had called Detective Cluney, who joined her at her office at the morgue.

"So, is this nurse a victim or a villain?" he asked

gruffly. He shifted uncomfortably, his large body looking outsized for the wooden chair on the opposite side of Haley's desk. He wasn't used to being on that side of the desk in another person's office, and his displeasure was apparent by the scowl on his face.

"I'm not sure," Haley said. "Perhaps both."

Detective Cluney removed a stub of a cigar from his pocket. "Mind if I smoke?"

"Actually," Haley started, "with all the chemicals and things in the morgue, it's not a good idea. I don't even have an ashtray to offer you."

A grunt was followed by the disappearance of the cigar stub back into a pocket Haley would never hope to stick a hand in.

"Those two dancers," Detective Cluney said with a lift of a bristled chin. "Do we have cause of death?"

"Not yet. Still waiting for laboratory results to come in. I have my suspicions."

"Poison, huh?"

"Yes."

"How does this nurse fit in?"

"Nurse Winkley attended both dance victims on the break before their deaths. Could be a coincidence, I suppose."

"Huh. Don't believe in coincidences, Doctor. What's her motive, then?"

"While I was waiting for Nurse Winkley at her apartment . . ." Haley did not say she'd been inside uninvited. "I took the liberty to look around."

Detective Cluney chuckled. "Liberty, huh? Fancy word for snooping."

"Be that as it may, I came across some personal information."

"Yeah? What?"

"I'd rather not say as it may have nothing to do with the case, only that it's possible that Bernice Prescott was also privy to it and may have been blackmailing Nurse Winkley."

"The dead girl was blackmailing the nurse?"

Haley nodded.

"Anything else?"

Haley's eyes went to the pot sitting on her desk. "I took this from Nurse Winkley's pantry. It's stew."

Detective Cluney raised a bushy brow. "You hungry, Doctor?"

"No. I have a hunch. I think Nurse Winkley's malaise may have been caused by something in the stew. I just want to get the laboratory to test it."

Tugging on his trousers, Detective Cluney rose

to his feet. "Just remember that's evidence. Be sure to let me know if anything's amiss."

"Certainly," Haley said.

After the detective left, she picked up the pot, took a fortifying breath, and was about to take it to the laboratory when Dr. Martin called out.

"Want me to take that for you, Doctor?"

"To the laboratory?"

"If that's where it's needed."

Haley pushed at the initial disappointment she felt, then embraced the relief at not having to see Dr. Murphy. Why was she behaving like such a school-girl around him? The best thing for all involved was for her to avoid him as much as possible.

"I'd appreciate it, Dr. Martin." Haley set the pot on his desk. "I'm curious if the same substance that killed Mr. Baines and Miss Prescott is also in this stew."

Dr. Martin attended to his new task immediately, leaving Haley alone in the morgue. She appreciated slower days. Most autopsies were straightforward affairs. Heart attacks. Cancers. Automobile accidents. Not all deaths required post-mortems, but sometimes, physicians or family members requested them for clarity.

A new body had come in that morning, waiting

in the cool cabinet. That was exactly what Haley needed right now. A familiar task that kept her mind and hands busy. She'd prepare the body, and as soon as Dr. Martin returned, they could get to the postmortem.

Haley washed down the steel table, set out the carving instruments, prepared the dishes that would receive the organs, and put a clean sheet of paper in her clipboard for notes.

After putting on her apron and headscarf, she washed her hands and then waited for Dr. Martin to return. Moving the body from the cool storage to the surgical table was infinitely easier with two people doing the task.

Not long afterward, Dr. Martin returned, and when the body, covered by a sheet, was settled on the table, he said, "Be right back, Doc. Nature calls."

Haley watched her assistant skip out of the morgue, then started on the Y incision, a procedure she'd done many times. Little blood marked her scalpel, as bleeding required a pumping heart.

A moment later, the door opened again, and Haley thought that Dr. Martin had made spectacular time. She looked up to tell him so, then stopped.

It wasn't Dr. Martin. Dr. Murphy stood near the door, staring at her.

Her vanity immediately flew into gear, her heart stammering as she thought of herself wrapped in a white apron, a scarf tied on her head to hold in flyaway curls, protective spectacles over her eyes, and a lightly bloodied scalpel in her hand.

"Dr. Murphy?"

"Yes, I see I'm interrupting. I only had a quick question."

"Regarding the stew?"

"No, nothing to do with work at all. I'm wondering if you'd be free to go to dinner with me sometime."

Haley blinked, her mind refusing to process the request. The hospital was full of pretty, *younger,* available nurses. Why on earth would he be asking *her,* a tall, extremely disinfected specimen of brains over beauty?

Dr. Martin breezed in before Haley could answer.

"Howdy, Dr. Murphy." Dr. Martin said. "Wanting to take in an autopsy, are you?"

"No," Haley said, a mite too forcefully. She swallowed then added carefully, "Dr. Murphy was just on his way out." She faced him with a veil of confidence. "I'm afraid I can't help you with your request, Doctor."

Dr. Murphy's very handsome eyes flashed with surprise, and Haley was certain he'd never been turned down before. Good. He was a little too big for his britches if he thought he could skip down the hall to her morgue for a personal matter.

"Very well," Dr. Murphy said. "Another time."

Haley watched as Dr. Murphy disappeared, her jaw dropping. *Another time?* Was that a challenge?

Dr. Martin cleared his throat. "Is everything all right, Doctor?"

Haley let out a breath, noting belatedly that she still held the scalpel out like a miniature sword. "Let's get going on this autopsy, shall we?"

17

*S*amantha considered her options as Johnny Milwaukee sat expectantly beside her on the bench in front of Quincy Market. Did she want to work on this story with him? She knew that she could do an excellent job of it on her own, but he was right; if they worked on it together, it would be a better piece, and the information he had just given her about Thelma Sikes's affair with Patrick Baines changed things. But she couldn't use any of it now unless she collaborated with Johnny. To do so wouldn't be fair to him after the investigative work he had done to uncover the whole thing.

"All right, Johnny, you're on," she said finally. "I'll let you know about anything that I get from Dr. Higgins, and you will pass on to me anything more you find out from your sources. Maybe we'll write the piece together; maybe not. We can decide that later."

"You got it, doll. This will be—" he stopped mid-sentence, his eyes squinting as he looked over her shoulder. "Wait, isn't that her?"

Samantha spun around in time to see the familiar figure of Thelma Sikes disappear into the entrance of Quincy Market.

Samantha shot to her feet. "We should go talk to her!"

They caught up to her at one of the many vegetable stalls as Mrs. Sikes perused the bins full of spring potatoes, onions, and early lettuce greens. Her cheeks were flushed, and her expression seemed flustered. She was examining a couple of wrinkly beets when she looked up and saw Samantha and Johnny approaching.

"Can you believe this?" she said as she held up the beets for Samantha and Johnny to see. "I remember when you could get these things firm and crisp. I can't believe we have to eat this junk." She shook them in the air, then threw the beets back into the bin.

"Hello, Mrs. Sikes. So nice to run into you like this." Samantha gestured toward Johnny. "You remember my colleague at the paper, Mr. Milwaukee? He spoke with you and Mr. Sikes at the marathon."

Thelma Sikes stared at Johnny as if she hadn't noticed him before, her lips curling into an appreciative smile. Her eyelids fluttered, softening her look. "Of course." She patted at her hair, then reached for his hand. "It's a pleasure to see you again, Mr. Milwaukee."

Samantha bristled at the unabashed flirtation, and Thelma, a married woman!

Johnny, always a charmer, said, "The pleasure's mine, Mrs. Sikes. We were wondering if you'd mind if we asked you just a few more questions."

"Not at all, but I don't see the point." She turned to Samantha, her countenance darkening. "I mean, I know there is a price for being a celebrity, but really, I thought Cyril and I gave you a pretty good interview for your paper already, didn't we? Hey, you aren't following me, are you?"

"Oh no, no. I leave that kind of thing to Mr. Milwaukee; he seems better at it." She couldn't help the jibe.

Johnny smirked at her and said, "We just happened to both be here at the same time and were talking in the plaza. We saw you coming into the market and thought we would say 'hiya.'"

"How serendipitous," Mrs. Sikes remarked.

"It was Mr. Sikes who spoke with me," Samantha said. "If you recall, you were not feeling well and had to lie down."

"Oh, sorry about that. Yes, I was still feeling drained from the marathon."

"Of course, I imagine it takes a while to recover from such a rigorous ordeal," Samantha offered.

"Okay, well, I guess we can have a little chat." Mrs. Sikes pulled up on her left sleeve to reveal a delicate-looking wristwatch. It was a casual sign of being comfortable financially, just like a car or an expensive necklace. Samantha guessed that the Sikeses had won more prize money than the average person made in a year.

Ignoring the other shoppers, who sidestepped them in search of suitable root vegetables, Samantha got right to it. "Did you and Mr. Sikes know any of the other couples personally from the marathon?"

"No, not really," she said after a moment of hesitation. "I mean, we'd met Patrick Baines once or twice."

"Oh? In what context?" Johnny asked.

"Investments. Cyril and Patrick were involved in

some of the same interests. I really know little about it, except that everyone lost a lot of money in the end. Just like a lot of people did during the panic."

"You don't know any specifics?" Johnny pressed. "Real estate? Stocks?"

"No, I don't. Besides, Cyril worked in pharmaceuticals. He only dabbled in investing." As if she were trying hard to focus, she blinked rapidly. "What has this got to do with the dance?"

Johnny inhaled, and Samantha had a feeling he was about to go in for the dirt. She would have engaged in a few more innocuous questions to build trust first, but she knew she couldn't control how Johnny conducted interviews.

"Well, probably nothing," Johnny began, "but in the interest of good journalism, which we are both committed to . . ." He waved a finger back and forth between Samantha and himself. "I'm always looking to get to the *real* story, and you see . . ." He cleared his throat. "My source tells me you both knew Patrick Baines quite well."

"What are you talking about?" Mrs. Sikes's blinking intensified. "What source?"

"I interviewed a former colleague of your husband's. He lives in a rundown shack in Roxbury and wasn't easy to find. His wife died last year of tuberculosis, and his health is not good, but he swears by what he told me. Apparently, he and Mr. Sikes were good friends, even after store hours. They used to grab a drink together at a bar down on Beacon."

"What? Who ... ?"

"Eddy Melbourne."

Mrs. Sikes gaped.

Johnny leaned in. "He has absolutely no reason to make this up, Mrs. Sikes."

"I am sure I don't know what you're talking about. I don't know an Eddy Melbourne."

"Well, he knows you. And I'll tell you what he told me—he said that Patrick Baines was a regular customer at the pharmacy where Mr. Sikes worked and that the two struck up a friendship."

Mrs. Sikes's mouth started working, her cheeks blushing. Samantha knew a woman in emotional distress when she saw one. Would riling her up like this give them the story they were after, or would she clam up and skedaddle?

Johnny was relentless. "Eventually, Mr. Baines convinced your husband to join him in a commercial real estate venture in Framingham, promising him all kinds of returns. Even after the blue-chip stocks started falling, Patrick Baines kept stringing Mr.

Sikes along, convincing him not to pull out and that the buyers were still lining up."

"I know nothing about any of that, and I think this so-called interview is over!" She glared at him, then spun to face Samantha. "Your friend is rude, Miss Hawke."

"The story gets even more interesting, doesn't it, Mrs. Sikes?" Johnny continued, stepping in behind her as the poor woman dodged other customers to get away. "Eddy Melbourne told me that one day while having drinks with Patrick Baines, Mr. Baines boasted about having an affair. With you."

Thelma Sikes froze, strength seemingly leaving her body as her shoulders slumped and her chin went down.

She turned slowly, tears running in rivulets down pale cheeks. "Yes, it's true. Please don't bring it up with Cyril. We're doing so well right now."

18

*W*ith the autopsy of the accident victim completed, the corpse was all sewn up—nothing amiss or suspicious this time, thankfully—and Haley cleaned her hands vigorously with a bar of lye soap.

The task had done what she'd hoped it would do: take her mind off the case, and beyond that, the new doctor. It was broaching what her British friend and former boss, Dr. Guthrie, would call teatime, and Haley debated if she should go home and work from her office there. She'd put a sandwich together—were there enough supplies in the pantry?—or sneak into the coffee shop, which was struggling to stay afloat during these challenging times when twenty cents for a cup of coffee was out of reach for many.

"Is it all right to shut the morgue down for the evening, Dr. Higgins?" Dr. Martin asked. "Or is there something else you'd like me to do?"

Haley considered her young assistant, eyes bright with the desire to do whatever the young did. "Date with Miss Mitzie?" she ventured.

"Only if you're not needing me, Doc."

Haley grinned. "Go on. No sense keeping a perfectly good specimen of the female gender waiting needlessly."

A broad smile stretched across Dr. Martin's face as he hopped to his feet and grabbed his hat and coat. "Thanks, Doc. See ya tomorrow."

Haley tidied her desk, picking up the phone when it rang.

"City morgue."

"Haley! I can't believe I caught you."

"Gerald." Haley settled into her chair and relaxed at the warmth of her friend's voice. "How are you?"

"I'm fine, though my stomach is hinting otherwise. Are you free to grab a bite to eat?"

"I was just thinking the same," Haley said. She missed his companionship and would love to tell him about her case like they had done as friends when his wife was still alive. "How about Waldorf's?"

"Give me thirty minutes."

Haley spent the next fifteen minutes finishing paperwork, then took a minute to check her hair in a mirror she kept in her desk drawer just for this purpose. Propping it on the desk, she fixed her curls, barely held in place with a myriad of bobby pins, then attached the hat society deemed necessary.

Slipping into a fitted wool jacket, she strapped her purse around her shoulder. She headed upstairs, but before she made it to the main entrance, she heard a familiar voice call her name.

"Dr. Higgins!"

She turned to the frantic expression of Mr. Regis North.

"Mr. North?"

"Hiya, Dr. Higgins. I know we barely know each other, but I can't get an answer from anyone here. It's Gladys."

"She's here?"

"Yes, they took her into a room and haven't come out. I'm going crazy with worry."

"I see. What happened exactly?"

"Well, it's this baby. It's making Gladys kind of crazy. Is that normal, Doctor? She's not very happy about it. I've caught her crying in the bathroom.

Shouldn't, you know, maternal instincts be kicking in?"

"Hormonal shifts brought on by pregnancy can create emotional instability in some women," Haley offered, but her mind was on the fact that Gladys North was in the hospital, and she'd love the chance to ask her a few questions.

"And she's got these strange cravings," Regis continued. "Really strange."

"How so?"

"Well, I caught her eating dirt! From the garden. Sucking on a flippin' turnip or something." Regis cocked his head. "Tell me that's normal?"

Haley had to concede it was on the odd side. "It should hardly merit a trip to the hospital."

"That's the thing. She started getting these stomach cramps." Regis lowered his voice. "I think her mind's in a bad way. I think she wants to get rid of the baby. That's what I think. She's hardly eating at all. Shouldn't she be hungrier? Eating for two and all that."

There were many old wives' tales circulating and plenty on how to end a pregnancy, like eating dangerous herbs or refusing to eat, "starving for two." With the state of the economy, many couples were worried about another mouth to feed. Haley eyed Regis.

"Are you happy about the baby?"

His shoulders slumped. "I suppose I will be; it's just rotten timing."

Haley shook her head, assuming what he was referencing. "The dance?"

Regis nodded.

"And a financial loss?"

"Hey, how d'you know about that? Oh yeah, you're friends with that Samantha broad, a friend of Gladys's. I know how hard it is for dames to keep their mouths shut."

Haley ignored the slight. "Let's see if I can find out something about Gladys."

Haley inquired at the reception desk and learned to which ward Gladys North had been assigned. With Mr. North on her heels, she found the room and went inside to find the attending doctor with Mrs. North. Her complexion was ashen and her breathing shallow.

"You need to take it easy, Mrs. North," Haley said. "I know you don't look like you're with child yet, but the first three months are the most precarious."

The doctor, recognizing Haley, shot her a questioning look.

She explained, "This is Mrs. North's husband, Regis. We share a mutual friend. I'm assuming the crisis has been averted."

"Yes, Dr. Higgins," he replied. "But as I was just telling our patient, she has to be more prudent with what she eats and not overexert herself."

"I'm sure Mr. North will see to it now."

Regis North frowned at his wife, who scowled in return, but gave the requisite nod.

Haley drew closer to the hospital bed. "Mrs. North, it's such a relief that you're all right."

"Yeah, I think it's just morning sickness or something. The baby doesn't like me. Making my stomach hurt." She looked at Regis point-blank. "Can you get me some soda crackers from the cafeteria?"

Regis seemed relieved to have a task to do and hurried away.

"What happened?" Haley asked. "Did you eat or drink something out of the ordinary?" She flashed a knowing look. "Hoping to change your circumstances, perhaps?"

"You're smart, Dr. Higgins," Mrs. North said, answering the question by not answering it. "Samantha always says you are."

"Samantha is a great person to have on your side. You're fortunate to have her as a friend."

"Yeah, I guess."

"Were you and Bernice Prescott friendly, by any chance?" Haley ventured. "Off the dance floor, at least."

"I suppose," Mrs. North said, looking bored. "All the contestants get to know each other, and we run into one another occasionally."

"Did you know Mildred Winkley before this marathon?"

Mrs. North narrowed her eyes. "Yeah. Only because we were in nursing school together for a while; I dropped out. Didn't have the stomach for it. So what?"

"No reason. Only, you might not know this, but she's a patient in this hospital now, too."

"Oh. Well, what d'ya know?"

"Can you think of a reason why someone might wish Nurse Winkley harm?"

Mrs. North scoffed. "Mildred Winkley may be a nurse, but she's no white lily."

"What do you mean by that?"

"She's not perfect, is what I'm saying."

"I see," Haley said. "Did Bernice Prescott know

that? I'm told that she and Nurse Winkley were close at one time."

"Not sure what you're getting at, Dr. Higgins."

Haley let out a tight breath. She was hoping Gladys North would jump at the chance to gossip. She could hardly bring up the scandalous teenage birth and subsequent cover-up. Mrs. North had hinted at knowing Nurse Winkley's secret. Could she be the nurse's blackmailer? If so, there was no sign of the extra money anywhere, at least not from what Samantha had told her. But the initials on the note were B.P. and it was Bernice Prescott who was dead, not Gladys North. Unless Nurse Winkley had accidentally poisoned the wrong dancer?

Haley forced a smile and answered the question. "Nothing, Mrs. North. I hope you feel better soon, and do listen to your doctor regarding your baby."

19

*A*s Thelma walked back into Quincy Market to finish her shopping, Johnny grabbed Samantha's arm.

"We should go interview Cyril before she gets home."

"Good idea." Sam stood. "Hard to tell, but we probably have an hour or so before she gets home."

They both raced to the bus stop. It was only a few minutes to the Sikeses's apartment from there.

As the bus rumbled down Court Street past the Old State House, Samantha turned to Johnny. "I wish you had told me all this before confronting the poor woman with the news that her secret is out."

"I never got the chance, doll."

"I guess not, but I wish you had eased into it a bit more. The woman was clearly distraught."

"Sometimes that happens in our line of work. You know that."

"I think your method might need some adjustments."

He raised his eyebrows at her. Obviously, he had worked as a reporter longer than she had, so taking advice from her, a woman, wasn't something he would easily swallow. Still, it needed to be said.

After disembarking, they rushed down the sidewalk with Johnny holding on to his fedora, and Sam clutching her purse. It was a half walk, half run gait, with several people on the street staring after them, no doubt wondering what the hurry was. Some even looked up worriedly at some windows in the three- and four-story buildings as Samantha and Johnny rushed along the street. Samantha remembered a story that *The Boston Daily Record* had published just a few months earlier. The article quoted statistics that the suicide rate in Boston had climbed dramatically in the last year.

Nobody climbing out on a window ledge today, she thought grimly.

They arrived at the front stoop, and Sam rang the buzzer. Both stood there catching their breath.

Samantha took some satisfaction in noticing that Johnny, who was taking off his fedora and mopping his forehead with a handkerchief, seemed more out of breath than her.

"There doesn't seem to be anyone home," he said after about twenty seconds had passed. He turned, stepped off the stoop, and looked down both directions of the street.

While he did that, Sam glanced over at what she remembered as the kitchen window. Cyril Sikes stood peering out while holding the curtain back slightly. With the other hand, he pointed at her.

She saw him mouth the words, "You, not him."

When he saw she'd understood, he backed away from the window, letting the curtain fall back into place.

"He's home, Johnny. He just motioned to me from the window."

"Why isn't he answering the door then?" Johnny's eyebrows furrowed together.

"He wants to talk to me, not you."

"What? Why?

"I don't know, but I will ask him." Samantha waved her hand dismissively at Johnny. "Now shoo. Go away. I'll meet you back at the office."

Johnny stood there for a moment, his disappointment clearly showing. "You shouldn't be in there alone with him," he said, finally.

"I'll get him to come outside. We'll talk on the stoop here."

He shook his head but then turned to go. Samantha knocked on the door again, and a moment later, Cyril Sikes, dressed in wool trousers cuffed at the hem and a knit V-neck pullover, slowly opened the door.

"He's gone, but I'm curious why you wouldn't talk to him," she said.

"Because I've read some of his columns. I like your writing style better. He always seems to be too dramatic, hinting at hidden scandals like he's got some kind of dirt on everybody."

Samantha didn't quite know how to respond to that one considering the circumstances.

"Are you going to stand out there all day? C'mon in."

"If it's all right with you, I would rather talk out here."

He paused for a minute and then nodded his head. "I see, I guess that's understandable. Thelma's not here right now." He stepped outside onto the stoop and closed the door behind him. They stood side by side as Samantha opened her bag and got her notes out.

"I assume you forgot to ask something in our last interview?"

"We just saw Thelma at Quincy Market."

"Oh? So why do you need to talk to me again? Not that I mind; besides, I suppose there are still a few things we can talk about."

"Actually, this might go in a different direction, and I am still trying to get a bead on it in some ways."

"How so?"

Samantha hesitated. She hadn't prepared herself for this line of questioning. The day's events had happened so fast, and in some ways, had been pulled along by Johnny, not her. But now, here she was, and the turn of events was simply too significant not to pursue because a suspected murder had been committed.

She was suddenly aware of the irony of berating Johnny just minutes earlier on the bus for being too direct.

She took a breath. "Mr. Sikes, I am just going to come out and ask the question."

"Sounds serious."

"Did you know that your wife was having an affair with Patrick Baines?"

He just stared ahead at the building across the street, his face unreadable.

"Who told you that?" he said finally, his voice even and without a hint of anger or surprise.

"Mr. Milwaukee found out from one of your old work colleagues."

"It was a while ago." He looked down at his feet . "The affair, I mean."

It wasn't the reaction Samantha had expected. "I must say, you don't seem all that surprised, Mr. Sikes."

"Oh, I'm surprised, all right. I'm surprised that it's with someone like you, a reporter— a *woman* reporter no less—that I am having this conversation."

"So, you knew?"

"I wouldn't say I knew with certainty, but I certainly suspected she was engaging in a liaison. I suppose Patrick Baines is as good a candidate as any."

He picked up a pebble lying on the stoop and tossed it into the street as he spoke.

"I'm confused, Mr. Sikes. If you suspected she was having an affair, didn't you ask her about it? Or at least, do some digging on your own?"

"I'm confused, *too*, Miss Hawke. I thought you

were writing a piece about the dance; maybe talk about what our strategies were, more about how we train and keep ourselves in shape. You seem to want to write about stuff that is no one's business but ours. That's disappointing, to say the least."

Samantha hesitated for a moment. She didn't know if she wanted to mention a suspected homicide, and there were possible motives to be uncovered.

"Thelma and I have a bit of an understanding on such matters. But *that* is not your business or anyone else's." He adjusted his suspenders. "Goodbye, Miss Hawke."

"But Mr. Sikes, can I just . . ."

He turned, the muscles along his jawline clenching, and walked back into the apartment, closing the door solidly behind him.

20

As Haley moved through the hospital toward the exit, her thoughts remained on Mrs. North. Unfortunately, troubled women in distress over being in the family way were common. Mrs. North had it better than most, as this was her first child. Many overwhelmed mothers had a child every other year, sometimes sooner. She knew of an Italian family near the docks where the poor wife was now expecting number fifteen. Sadly, three of her children had been buried.

Though Mrs. North needed more care, Haley knew Mr. North would check her out before the day was through. Very few could afford the cost of a hospital stay, and Haley had heard grumbling from the hospital administrations on how the bills weren't getting paid. One even insinuated that the electricity might have to be turned off at intervals. Haley had pointed out how that would be a precarious situation with bodies lying in cold storage in the morgue.

Her mind was so preoccupied that she, rather unbelievably, ran into Dr. Murphy, again!

"Please excuse me," she said, smoothing out her jacket. "I really must keep my head up while walking."

Dr. Murphy smiled. "I can't say that I mind. You looked deep in thought. Perhaps a cup of tea with someone new to the neighborhood is exactly what you need." Few men needed to duck their chins to look Haley in the eyes, but Dr. Ronan Murphy was an exception.

"I don't—"

"You're not going to let me eat alone, are you? I'm counting on your Irish hospitality," he added with a twinkle in his clear blue eyes, "You're still Irish, eh?"

Haley found herself relaxing around Dr. Murphy's jovial manner. "For sure, though I was born in Boston. My grandparents immigrated from Ireland. My parents had a farm outside the city."

Before Haley realized it, she was strolling out of the hospital with Dr. Murphy, who was regaling her with stories from the homeland. By the time they entered the coffee shop on the corner, she was laughing.

How long had it been since she'd enjoyed a hearty laugh? Too long, by her measure.

The café was long and narrow, larger than it appeared from the street, with a high counter lined with tall wooden chairs down one wall and a row of tables set for four along the other. Haley and Dr. Murphy claimed the last empty table, second in from the window. Shortly after they were settled, a waitress approached, coffees and tuna sandwiches were ordered, and water was set on the table.

"I was raised on fish and potatoes; most Dublin kids were," Dr. Murphy said as they waited for their food. "No one could fry up a kipper like my ma. That and stew and soda bread, but there's plenty of that to be found around here."

Haley smiled. "It's become a staple."

The coffees and sandwiches arrived, and after a bite, Dr. Murphy continued. "The thing I miss the most is the hills of heather in the spring. Deep purple-clad hills, so beautiful when washed with dewy sunshine, it takes your breath away."

"Quite clearly, you're still in love with Ireland," Haley said. "What brought you to Boston?"

"You think times are tough here? Ireland depends too much on agriculture and lost out on export sales after the panic. Poverty and homelessness are widespread."

"It's not much better here."

"Oh, but it is. There's still opportunity to be had, even if it's harder to grab on to now. Besides," he grinned rakishly, "it seems pretty Irish lassies can be found here as there."

Haley stared back without smiling, wondering what Dr. Murphy was playing at. If Haley was anything, she was a realist. She knew she didn't possess the beauty and feminine wiles bestowed on Samantha. She was a scientist, cared little about fashion and what people thought of her looks (mostly), and on top of that, was a tomboy, preferring frogs to frocks, baseball bats to knitting needles, and golf clubs to parasols.

Dr. Murphy sat back and studied her like she was a foreign specimen.

"You're different from most ladies with whom I share tea."

"I'm told that a lot," Haley said flatly.

"I mean that as a compliment." Dr. Murphy reached over to pat her hand, an act of kind companionship that with another person would never be misconstrued for anything else. But with this man, Haley's level of attraction betrayed her. She didn't have time for a romantic fling—for that was undoubtedly what a dalliance with Dr. Murphy would be—she was married to her work. Not only that, but it was also never a good idea to get involved with a coworker. Look at the troubles Samantha had with Mr. Milwaukee.

And besides, there was Gerald.

Gerald!

Haley shot upright. She'd forgotten about Gerald. Frantically, she checked her watch. Her scheduled meeting for supper was nearly an hour past.

"Is everything all right?" Dr. Murphy said, looking sincerely alarmed.

"Yes, no, it's just, I forgot—"

Before Haley could push away from the table, a shadow formed above, and when she looked up and saw who it was, she wished the earth would split and swallow her whole.

"Haley?" Gerald said. With salt-and-pepper hair that was more salt than pepper, Gerald looked old enough to be Dr. Murphy's father. Deep crow's feet fanned out from brown eyes, which were awash with a blend of hurt and confusion.

"Gerald." Haley sprung to her feet.

It was natural for Gerald to search for her if he hadn't found her at home. She came here often and many times with Gerald as her companion. "I'm so sorry. I got caught up with a patient and completely forgot."

"A patient?" he said dryly. "You work with the dead."

His gaze landed on Dr. Murphy, so youthful and handsome and virile. "Apparently, I'm wrong."

"This is Dr. Murphy," Haley said, striving for professionalism. "He's new to General. Head of the laboratories. Dr. Murphy, this is my good friend, Dr. Gerald Mitchell, a geriatric specialist."

Dr. Murphy stood and offered his hand. "Pleased to meet you, Dr. Mitchell. I'm always happy to make the acquaintance of new colleagues. I gather Dr. Higgins forgot her diary. You'll have to forgive her. I practically swooped her away. Finding a friendly and helpful face is a relief when one is new to a city and workplace."

"It's a simple mistake," Haley said quickly. "I was actually seeing a friend of Samantha's who was brought in, just as I was about to leave to meet you."

Forever a gentleman, Gerald remained

composed. "I'm sorry to hear about the lady's poor health. Might I inquire of Nurse Winkley?"

"Of course. She's still in a comatose state, but her doctor has hope that she'll awaken soon. Let's make our way to Waldorf's, and I'll fill you in on everything."

To Dr. Murphy, she said, "You'll forgive me for leaving early? I'll pay on my way out."

"Please allow me to pick up the tab," Dr. Murphy said. "It's the least I can do for mucking up your date."

*a*s Samantha crossed School Street toward City Hall, she glanced up to her left to see Benjamin Franklin looking down at her disapprovingly. "None of your business, Mr. Franklin," she muttered toward the eight-foot-high bronze statue.

Josiah Quincy, mayor of Boston over one hundred years before, stared down from his bronze perch to her right. He looked aghast as he clutched his robe protectively as if to say, "Is nothing safe from the prying eyes of the press?"

Samantha remembered reading about the infamous incident in 1825 when Josiah Quincy had refused to close the district known as the "Beehive," an area renowned for its brothels, despite demands from much of Boston's population to do so. As a result, two hundred working-class men tore it to the ground piece by piece. The press helped circulate rumors that Quincy himself was a regular patron of the brothels, thus his reticence to close the district. Of course, this was never proven.

Perhaps Mr. Quincy had reason to distrust the press. To prove that not all journalists were self-serving, Samantha gave a little wave to Mayor Quincy as she hurried past and up the columned steps into Boston's City Hall.

After consulting the building's directory, she made her way through the massive structure to the Registry of Public Records Office. A clerk showed her how to find the files she was looking for: In this instance, the record of marriage for Cyril and Thelma Sikes.

Fred Hall's biography of the couple for the interest piece on the dance marathon had stated the Sikeses were married in 1925, so Samantha began her search with that year. Unfortunately, she didn't know the month, only that they were married in Boston. After about thirty minutes of searching, she found the registry with their names and carried it to a viewing table at the far end of the room.

Samantha found a copy of the marriage certificate with the heading Registry Department of the

City of Boston, County of Suffolk inside the folder. It was made out for Cyril James Sikes and Thelma Glenda Sikes (née Johansson), dated 1925.

When Cyril had spoken the words "special arrangement," she had had a hunch that perhaps they were living common law: an arrangement many would consider scandalous, and not the information a celebrity couple would want to get out. Samantha could understand the temptation to carry out the ruse. There were certain advantages to being a married couple, such as renting an apartment, traveling, and gaining public favor as a celebrity dance team. But it looked like her hunch was off.

Samantha let out a tired breath as she stared at the certificate. Why the strange reaction from Cyril Sikes? After writing the details in her notebook, Samantha drummed her fingers on the table and glanced about the room's high ceilings. The aisle next to the marriage records was labeled "Records of Annulment and Divorce." She looked up at the clock on the wall. This might take a while.

This time she didn't even have a year to go by, but after about two hours, she finally saw the name "Sikes" written on one of the files. Inside the manila folder was a copy of a divorce certificate, dated 1928.

Special arrangement, indeed. Thelma's affair

with Patrick Baines certainly constituted a reason for divorce. It also lent itself as a motive for murder.

Samantha was ready to hash the case out with Haley, telling all she'd learned so far. After putting the files back where they belonged, Samantha started toward the exit door when another thought hit her. She rechecked the time. She had about an hour before she needed to pick up Talia. There would be far more guesswork this time because she didn't even have a year to go by. She could start ten years back and work towards the present.

Johnny Milwaukee would have been twenty-three years old at that time.

Samantha sat at the viewing table, twisting a strand of blond hair around one finger, and wondered about the ethics of what she was about to do. Prying into someone else's life, especially if it had nothing to do with any story she was working on, was wrong. But Johnny's response to her accusation that he didn't know what it was like to care for anyone but himself, had stuck in her mind like mental glue. For an unguarded moment, something honest had flashed behind his eyes.

Didn't matter. She smoothed her skirt and poised herself to stand. Johnny's past was none of her business.

She'd only gone a few steps when the devil on her shoulder whispered, "If you are going to work closely with Johnny on this story, and perhaps others in the future, you have a right to know if there are any skeletons in his closet."

Once again, she headed down the aisle of marriage records, following a newshound hunch.

Johnny wasn't a story.

She would only make a quick search. Probably she'd find nothing. No harm done. Besides, she didn't have enough time to dig deep.

Because she now had some experience with the filing system that the registry employed, she was able to go a little faster this time. Soon she was staring down at a file with a label that made her heart beat faster: "Milwaukee."

It was an unusual name, but it wasn't impossible for it to belong to someone else. Maybe even unrelated.

She returned to the viewing table with the file. Tapping her fingers on the envelope, she blew air out of her cheeks.

Put it back.

"I'll just see if it's even about Johnny," she murmured, and her long nails retrieved the paper inside.

Samantha's heart pounded in her chest. This was Pandora's box. Now that her eyes had seen it, she could never go back. Her fingers quivered as they gripped the certificate dated July 1922, which chronicled the marriage of one Jonathon George Milwaukee to a Karen Faith O'Sullivan.

"Okay, so what. Big deal. He's been married."

But he didn't want anyone to know. Why else did no one know?

Still, no big secret, really. Samantha herself had also been married. The topic would come up in conversation, eventually, in a regular manner. She'd just have to keep this knowledge to herself until Johnny decided to share it with her. Over time, with how their friendship was going, it would likely come up.

While putting the file back into the envelope, she stopped when she saw a handwritten note fall out. In black ink, it read, Addendum—please see Death Certificate 14556.

Oh, no.

She should stop now, but there was no way she could. Her strength as a journalist was also her weakness.

Samantha quickly found the aisle entitled, Records of the Public Health Service, putting the file back where it belonged. Since she already had the certificate number, it only took a few moments to find it.

She felt her eyes start to well up as she read the certificate of death dated February 18, 1923, for Karen Faith Milwaukee. The cause of death was stated as "complications during childbirth; unnamed female infant, stillborn."

Samantha's shoulders slumped under the weight of Johnny's secret, heavier still as it was something she had no right to know.

"Oh, Johnny. I'm so sorry."

22

*H*aley and Samantha shared an illicit nightcap in the comfort of their living room. The chill of March still allowed for a crackling fireplace.

Mrs. Berrymaple waved from the French door that opened into the corridor. "I'll be off now if you no longer need me."

"Thank you so much," Haley said. She had excused herself from dinner, having lived through an agonizing meal with Gerald, where she couldn't stop herself from profusely apologizing.

"You're beginning to make me think you actually have something to be sorry for," Gerald had said after her last episode.

"Dinner was lovely," Samantha added. "You don't have to do this for us, you know."

"Would you let an old lady eat alone?" was Mrs. Berrymaple's reply. "I'll see you tomorrow if you're not sick of me."

"Never," Samantha said.

After the door sounded with a click, Samantha let out a sigh of gratitude. "She is a godsend. I'm so exhausted by the time I get home that I barely have enough energy to help Talia with her schoolwork and get her ready for bed, much less put together a decent meal."

"We can make the arrangement official," Haley said. "Hire her properly."

"I can't—"

"It's for me, not for you," Haley said. "I like to come home to a good supper and go to bed with a clean kitchen. No offense to your cooking. Or house-keeping."

"None taken." Samantha raised her glass. "To Mrs. Berrymaple." After a sip, she asked the obvious. "As a fan of Mrs. B.'s cooking, I couldn't help but notice your absence."

Haley pinched her eyes shut. "I made a fool of myself today."

Samantha leaned in, wide-eyed. "Oh? Fess up."

"It's embarrassing."

"I've got an embarrassing story too. You go first."

Haley considered her eager friend. "It's not a news story."

"Of course not. What do you take me for?" Samantha crossed her heart. "I promise anything spoken in this room on this night is off the record."

"Very well." Haley huffed. "Like I said, this is embarrassing, and I don't want you to make a big deal out of it."

"Oh, oh, oh. Let me guess. Does it have anything to do with the new handsome doctor?"

Haley folded her free arm across her chest. "That's it. I'm not talking."

"Oh, come on, Haley. Let me live vicariously through you."

"He asked me out, and I said no."

Samantha glared with disappointment. "That's it? That's your embarrassing news?"

"Well, that's not all of it. Later, he asked me out again, and I said yes."

Samantha hooted. "You had a dinner date with Dr. Handsome!"

"No, just coffee, but I forgot about the dinner date I had with Gerald."

"Uh-oh."

"And he found me at the coffee shop with Dr. Handsome."

"Yikes. So, wait, you left Dr. Handsome to have dinner with Dr. Geriatric." Haley scowled, and Samantha made a quick revision. "I mean Dr. Mitchell."

"I felt so silly, getting swept away by a pretty boy. Me. At my age."

"You talk like you're an old maid."

"I'm older than him."

"By how much?"

Haley was going to say she didn't know, but of course, she'd confirmed the statistic. "Five years."

"And how much older is Dr. Mitchell than you?"

"Fifteen years."

Samantha whistled. "I don't know about you, but I see a double standard."

"Anyway, I left Dr. Murphy and went for dinner with Gerald, and it was awkward. I fear Gerald feels a little insecure, and I certainly didn't help matters."

"You're not married to him," Samantha said. "You're not even officially dating. You're free to see other men."

"I don't want to see other men," Haley blustered. "I don't want to see any men. I'm busy with my work, which takes me to why I was upstairs at the hospital. Regis North brought Gladys in."

Samantha jerked upright. "Is she all right?"

Haley considered her next words. She didn't want to gossip or spread a presumption she had about Samantha's friend. "I think she's mentally overwrought. Nothing a good night's rest can't cure. But—"

"But?"

"I have a suspicion that Gladys did this to herself."

"What do you mean?" Samantha said, then understanding dawned. "Do you think she's trying to end her pregnancy?"

"It would be worth checking in on her," Haley replied.

"I'll do that." Samantha strolled to the fireplace, picked up the poker, and gave the logs a push.

Haley plucked the pins out of her curls and ran her fingers through her hair. "Your turn, Sam. I'm waiting to hear about your embarrassing moment."

Samantha returned to her spot on the couch and pulled her feet underneath her. "It's more of a shameful thing than embarrassing. I had no witnesses."

Haley noted Samantha's reticent tone. "What happened?"

"I went to the city hall to look up something about the Sikeses. It turns out they're divorced."

"Interesting," Haley said. "Why are they passing themselves off as still married?"

"My guess is the ruse is good for business. They are celebrities in some circles. Johnny discovered that Thelma Sikes had once had an affair with Patrick Baines—"

"And the plot thickens."

"She begged us not to tell Mr. Sikes, but when I spoke with him, I got the distinct impression he already knew."

"So, they each have a motive to kill Mr. Baines. Mrs. Sikes didn't want her ex-husband to know about the affair, and Mr. Sikes wanted revenge—or to prevent a romance from reigniting."

"Their reputations are at stake," Samantha added, "which could affect their endorsements."

"When do you get to the shameful part?" Haley asked with a grin.

Samantha sipped the last of her drink. "Now. At the city hall, after I'd checked up on the Sikeses, I decided to do a little digging on Johnny."

Haley shot her a look. "Why would you do that?"

"Something he said today made me think there's more to him than meets the eye. And I was right."

"Are you sure you want to tell me what you found?"

Samantha shook her head. "No. That would make me an even worse person than I am. I'm only confessing that I did it when I shouldn't have."

"I'm assuming you found something out you wish you didn't know."

"I did. But it's nothing on Johnny. He's actually a better man than I'd given him credit for."

"I see."

"What do you see?"

"That whatever you discovered today has made your feelings for Johnny grow deeper."

Samantha's mouth opened in protest, then clamped shut.

"It doesn't matter. I'm like you. Married to my work. And I have Talia. Any man would just complicate matters, especially Johnny."

"I'm glad that's settled," Haley said. "Let's get back to the case. Cyril Sikes has a motive; Thelma Sikes has a motive."

"At least when it comes to Patrick Baines. What do they have against Bernice Prescott?"

"Other than the threat that she and Regis North might push them off the winner's pedestal?"

"Regis is still alive," Samantha offered.

"True. But it looks like Miss Prescott made an enemy out of Nurse Winkley."

"Oh? Do tell!"

"I will." Haley looked Samantha in the eye. "However, I'm holding you to all things stated here tonight as being off the record."

Samantha leaned in. "What did you find out?"

"I visited Nurse Winkley today, and, well, she'd left the door unlocked."

"You went inside?"

"Just to wait for her. And yes, I had a little look," Haley offered. "Consider this my tale of shame. I found a shoebox with evidence that Nurse Winkley had a child out of wedlock, now being raised by her parents."

"Hardly unique," Samantha said.

"No, but a secret, nonetheless. One that I suspect Bernice knew. I found a blackmail note among Nurse Winkley's things signed with the initials B.P."

"Ah," Sam sang. "Motive. Did you confront her? Do you think she killed Miss Prescott to keep her secret safe?"

"I don't know. She came home while I was there, but before we could properly converse, she collapsed. She's convalescing in the hospital as we speak."

"Oh dear."

"Her doctor has reassured me that Nurse Winkley will recover. However—I think she might've been poisoned."

Samantha stood, reaching to the ceiling as she stretched out her back. "How many poisoners do we have among us?"

"Historically, poison is the most common means of committing murder," Haley said. "Only recently have tests been developed that can identify poisonous substances found at crime scenes or previously consumed by the deceased." Haley brought a finger to her chin. "Mr. Farber worked with gas and poisons during the war."

"True," Samantha said. "But so far, we haven't come up with a motive."

"And your friend, Regis North," Haley began. "I hate to say it, but you've mentioned he was once a botanist. He'd know how to make a plant-based poison."

"Oh, I really hope it isn't him," Samantha said. "Poor Gladys has had such rotten luck with him as it is. But don't forget that Mr. Sikes was a pharmacist. He'd also be knowledgeable about poisons."

"Too many qualified killers," Haley said. She tugged on her trousers as she got to her feet. "Let's sleep on it, shall we? Tomorrow is another day."

23

Samantha regarded her daughter, who sat across from her at the kitchen table, with some amusement. Talia was busily munching on her breakfast of Kellogg's Corn Flakes and concentrating hard. She'd placed the white-and-green box in front of her bowl, reading the sides of it while she ate.

"What's this mean?" Talia mumbled, her mouth half full of cereal. She turned the box and pointed with her spoon at the small print.

"It's a warning," Samantha said. "It says that if you talk with your mouth full, you risk being thought of as rude."

For a second, Talia stopped chewing and looked at her mom before a small smile crept onto her face, her cheeks bulging.

"It does not."

"Doesn't it?"

"What does it *mean*?"

"It's just legal mumbo jumbo."

Talia pushed her lips out and nodded, having heard the excuse before. She stuffed another spoonful of milk and flakes into her mouth while turning the box back toward her.

Mrs. Berrymaple, who'd been given a key to the apartment, walked into the kitchen with a small box of vegetables in her arms.

"You were out shopping already?" Samantha asked.

"No. This was sitting in front of the door in the hall. A few potatoes, some celery, carrots, onions." She rifled through the box. "A few other roots. Everything you might need to make a good stew."

"Haley must have ordered it," Samantha said. "I guess she's already thinking about supper. That woman's mind is far more orderly than mine, that's for sure."

Mrs. Berrymaple agreed. "Probably comes with her line of work."

Talia lifted her bowl to her face and slurped down the last of the sweet milk before putting the bowl down with a clunk. She then dramatically wiped her mouth with her forearm.

"Ahhh!" She made a sound like she had just polished off a huge drink.

"Talia!" Samantha said with a mix of horror and amusement. "Is that how a young lady should finish her meal?"

"I don't know, but that's what Billy Lorenzo does all the time."

"You don't have to do the same thing Billy Lorenzo does. I'm sure he would agree."

"I don't. If I did, I would let out a good burp right now, but I am a lady, so I won't."

"Thank goodness!" Samantha said, sharing a grin with Mrs. Berrymaple. "Now, go finish getting ready for school. We don't want to be late."

To SAMANTHA'S SURPRISE, she arrived at the front door of *The Boston Daily Record* just as Mr. Farber was coming out.

"Mr. Farber?"

"Miss Hawke."

"Are you here to report on a story?"

Mr. Farber guffawed. "Don't worry, little lady. I didn't give anything juicy to your handsome sidekick.

Just bought a bit of advertising." He rubbed his thick palms together. "The next marathon's in Newton." He grinned crookedly. "You and your partner should sign up."

"I don't have a partner, Mr. Farber. I work on my own."

"Ah, ya, sure."

"It doesn't concern you that two contestants at your last event were murdered?"

"Hey, now that's not proven, and I don't appreciate you spreading slanderous rumors."

Mr. Farber's smarmy smile told Samantha that the organizer enjoyed the attention. Any publicity was good publicity.

"I imagine you've got advertisers lining up now," she said.

"No better way to get hundreds of eyeballs on something you want to sell."

Would the man sabotage his contestants to gain advertising dollars? Maybe he hadn't meant for them to die, but the effect was the same. And the man showed the low regard he had for human life by organizing such savage events.

He placed a palm on her shoulder. "You're young, look to be in good shape, and *purty* as can be. The paying public would eat you up. Think what you could do with a grand!"

Samantha stepped back, relieving herself of his grip. "I have to decline, Mr. Farber."

He shrugged and walked away.

Samantha pulled on the door handle but called out before entering. "Mr. Farber, is it true that you have experience working with poisons?"

Mr. Farber scowled, waving her off as he jaywalked across the street.

Inside, Samantha went through the messages, including, to her surprise, a note from Gladys North inviting her for lunch. At least that meant her friend was no longer in the hospital, and Samantha swallowed a lump of guilt that she hadn't even made the time to check in on her.

There were also instructions from Mr. August with an assignment to fit in this weekend, and Samantha's mood darkened.

"Hey, doll," Johnny said as he walked into the office. "Why so glum?" He stopped at her desk to stare over her shoulder. Seeing the editor's note, he picked it up and said, "Ah. I get it. Back to the fluff pieces, huh? Knit sweaters?"

"It's the latest fashion trend," Samantha said with a note of resignation. "Woolworth's department store is having a special promotion in their knitting and crochet section on Saturday. I have to cover it."

"Golly!" Johnny said with a tease. "I'm gonna mark that on my calendar."

"You should. They're giving away peach-colored candles as a door prize, as well as several new patterns for winter scarves. You could use a new winter scarf, I bet."

"Only if you knit it for me, doll face."

Samantha huffed. "Not on your life."

"See the bright side," Johnny said. "You'll get paid to sit around in Woolworth's for an afternoon bumping gums with all the housewives."

Samantha threw her pencil on the desk in disgust. "What's your next assignment after the murder case at the dance is finished?"

"Dunno. Haven't got one yet."

"Whatever it is, I'm sure it will be more exciting than mine."

"Maybe I'll ask Archie if I can trade ya."

Samantha smiled. "Would you?"

"Sure. Course he wouldn't buy it."

Since discovering Johnny's past, Samantha viewed him in a new light. Instead of an arrogant showman, she saw a man putting on a front of bravado and swagger. Those things were part of his charm, as irritating as they could be, but now she knew there was more to him, and she was intrigued.

"What are you staring at me like that for?" Johnny's eyebrows furrowed together. "You all right?"

"No . . . I mean, yes. I'm all right." She turned away and busied herself with her notes. "No . . . nothing's wrong."

Johnny leaned on the edge of her desk, whipped out a cigarette, and lit it. "What did you find out from Sikes?" Johnny blew smoke away from Samantha toward the ceiling.

Recovering from her earlier blunder, she said coyly, "Some interesting stuff."

"C'mon, Sam. You're not going to clam up on me now, are ya? It was me who got the dirt on Thelma Sikes."

Samantha picked up her pencil and tapped it on the desk. "He reacted strangely when I mentioned the affair," she said.

"I would imagine he would. No fellow likes to be put on the spot like that. But, strange? In what way?"

"He said something about an arrangement. With his wife."

Johnny lifted his chin. "Oh? What kind of arrangement?"

"He didn't come out and say, but I followed a

hunch. I went to City Hall and looked up their marriage records."

Johnny snapped his fingers and jabbed one at her. "I would have thought of doing that —eventually."

"I'm sure."

"Let me guess." Johnny's eyebrows jumped. "You didn't find any. They're not really hitched."

"Oh, they got hitched all right . . ." Samantha took pleasure in drawing out the suspense. If she had to kowtow to her boss and do that boring fluff piece, she would get her entertainment where she could.

"Hmm, so . . . ?"

"They are also divorced." Samantha watched as understanding came into his eyes.

Johnny whistled. "Since when?"

"1928."

"Faking being married to preserve their reputation?" Johnny puffed on his cigarette, then rubbed his chin. "Why not just get remarried and avoid a potential scandal?"

"My guess, they don't really like each other outside of dancing," Samantha said. "Thelma Sikes behaved very strangely, detached from real life, like she was on something, then left the room before my 'interview' even started."

"Okay, this is good, this is *really* good." Johnny stood up from leaning on the desk. "The readers are gonna eat this up!"

"Wait. There's more. The date on the divorce papers could very well line up with the time when Thelma had the affair with Patrick Baines."

Johnny stared at Samantha with nothing short of admiration in his eyes. "Archie is wasting you on fluff pieces."

Samantha agreed, but before she could say anything, Johnny went on.

"I can see the headline." He waved a hand in front of his face as he imagined it. "Hanky-Panky Motive for Murder: Marathon dangerous place for two-timers."

He sauntered back to his desk, butting his cigarette out with a flourish, and Samantha bit her cheek to keep from smiling. She had to be careful: though she now had a renewed appreciation for the man, it didn't mean she could fall for him.

She refocused her attention on her work and picked up the note from Gladys. Scribbling a response saying she accepted her friend's invitation, she searched for a free messenger boy and instructed him to deliver it, pronto.

24

"*M*orning, Doc," Dr. Martin said, his greeting even more exuberant than usual.

"Good morning, Dr. Martin," Haley returned cheerily. "Can I take it by your sunny disposition that your date with Mitzie went well?"

Dr. Martin grinned crookedly. "She's a sweet patootie. How about you?"

Not understanding the context of the question, Haley blinked in confusion. "What do you mean, how about me?"

"With Dr. Mitchell?" An impish grin formed on his face. "Or is it Dr. Murphy now?"

"Dr. Martin!"

Her assistant's expression turned from smug to

horror. "Forgive me, Doc. I've forgotten my place. I'm only going by what I—you know what, never mind. Let's see. What's on the agenda? Any new bodies coming our way?"

Haley scowled. "You're only going by what you *heard?*"

"Dr. Higgins," his voice implored. "The coffee shop on the corner is frequented by hospital staff. Surely you noticed?"

Haley had, of course, but thought her position behind the high walls of the booth had concealed her. Besides, she'd hardly caught the attention of the staff before.

Before blasted Dr. Murphy. It ruffled her feathers to know that her colleagues were having fun at her expense.

Dr. Martin, apparently daunted by Haley's silence, prattled on. "Don't mind those silly nurses. They're just unhappy that *you* snagged the pretty doctor."

Haley heard the slight emphasis on the word "you."

"I've *snagged* no one. I was simply cordial toward a new member of staff. Nothing more. Now can we please get to work?"

"Yes, ma'am."

Haley soothed her nerves with a cup of tea, an indulgence she'd grown to appreciate during her time spent in London. It reminded her of her dear friend Ginger, and she could hear her voice with a hint of laughter: *You have to admit, Haley, it is rather funny. One must learn to laugh at oneself on occasion.*

Haley rolled her shoulders. Her faux love triangle was a mite hilarious. She'd have to write Ginger and tell her all about it.

The morgue phone rang, and Haley let Dr. Martin answer. Though her initial mortification was easing, she still hadn't forgiven her assistant for his impertinence. Soon, Dr. Martin knocked tentatively on the door. "Not to bother you, Doc, but that was the laboratory. The test results on Baines, Prescott, and Winkley are in."

"Fantastic. Be a peach and fetch them for me."

Dr. Martin hopped to his task, and Haley was thankful she had him to send. Avoidance of Dr. Murphy was high on her priority list.

Finally, she would know the cause of death. Her mind went to their list of suspects, landing on Thelma Sikes. She was most likely a cocaine addict; she liked cooking, so she was a good candidate for spiking Nurse Winkley's stew.

Dr. Martin returned with an envelope. "Here it is, Doc."

As Haley used a letter opener to break the seal, Dr. Martin continued nervously. "Um, I'm sorry for before. I stepped over a line."

Haley shot him a glance. "It's forgotten. Now, let's see what we have here."

She pulled out the report, her eyes quickly scanning the document. "Water hemlock."

"Hemlock?" Dr. Martin returned.

"*Water* hemlock. It grows in streams and boggy meadows. Deadly for cattle and people alike. The whole plant is toxic, but the roots are especially so. It's also known as poison parsnip."

"Could be confused with real parsnips," Dr. Martin mused.

"Or carrots."

Dr. Martin raised his chin. "Hence the similar odor found in the mouth cavities of the corpses."

"Yes. The root is fleshy and white, a reasonable facsimile to parsnips, but smelling more like carrots. This was how the stew was poisoned."

"What about the dancers? Did they eat stew?"

Haley shook her head. "All the dancers were fed the same meals. In that instance, the water hemlock must've been boiled down, with the reduced water carrying enough of the poison that a few drops put into the victims' water glasses were sufficient to do the job. The toxin would've taken effect, causing seizures within fifteen minutes of ingesting it."

Which a botanist would know.

Regis North!

Haley hurried to her office and called *The Boston Daily Record*.

"Please connect me to Samantha Hawke."

After a moment on hold, she was told that Samantha had left the building.

"Do you know where she went?"

"She had several messages today," the receptionist replied.

"Were any of them of a personal nature?"

"Let me see. Ah, yeah, there's one from a Mrs. North. She invited Miss Hawke for lunch."

"Oh, I'm so glad you could make it." Gladys smiled at Samantha as she stood in the open doorway, still looking a little wan. "Come on in. Regis is out running errands."

"I'm sorry for not coming to see you in the hospital," Samantha said as she entered the apartment. "I only just learned from Dr. Higgins that you'd been ill."

"Oh, think nothing of it." Gladys took Samantha's jacket and hung it on a coat rack beside the front door. "I was only in there for a short time anyways."

Samantha nodded pointedly at Gladys's midsection. "Nothing serious, I hope?"

"Just a bit of indigestion. Felt worse than it was. Take a seat."

Samantha claimed an upholstered barrel chair and put her feet up on the matching ottoman. Although certainly not new, the set appeared to be in good shape and of higher quality than most other pieces in the living room. A remnant from better days, it was a reminder of how things had changed for so many people over the last few years.

"I've made soup and cucumber and mustard sandwiches," Gladys called as she entered the kitchen. "Regis cleared out the rest of the veggies from the winter garden. Wants to plant for spring soon, so I thought I'd throw the last of them in a pot."

Samantha followed Gladys and took a seat at the table already set with bowls and spoons, and two glasses of water. "Soup sounds lovely," she said. It was the time of year when the fall harvest dwindled but new spring offerings were yet to come. And in these tough times, everyone ate what was set before them.

Gladys carried over a pot of soup, ladling out a portion for each of them, then returned with two plates carrying a sandwich for each.

"I hope the soup isn't bitter," Gladys said. "No tomatoes to sweeten it up."

Samantha blew on her soup, sipping carefully. She agreed with Gladys that the soup was less than stellar, but she sipped it anyway to be polite.

Gladys nibbled on her sandwich, her gaze drifting.

"Are you sure you're well?" Samantha inquired gently. "I do hope you're not doing too much."

"I'm fine. I guess the marathon took a little more out of me than I thought it did this time." Unsmiling, she patted her still-flat stomach. "This is to blame."

Gladys didn't appear happy about the new addition, and Samantha recalled Haley's suspicion that she might have ended up in the hospital after an effort to end it on her own.

As Samantha sipped her soup, she searched for a radio or gramophone, something she could suggest they turn on for background noise. She and Gladys were friends but not close, and for some reason, this visit was plagued with stilted conversation. Unfortunately, there wasn't a radio or music-maker in sight.

As she continued to chew on her sandwich and slurp her soup, Samantha noted that much of what was personal, apart from the furniture, was gone. No wall hangings or ornaments, just one lone record leaning against the back of an empty bookshelf.

"Where is your gramophone?" Samantha asked, blinking as her vision blurred. She really needed to get more sleep. "And records? Are you and Regis moving?"

Gladys's eyes darkened. "We had to sell them, Sam. For money. Can you believe the Sikeses offered to buy them!" She snorted. "Over my dead body!"

Samantha reeled at the vitriol spewing from her friend's mouth but completely understood the effects of poverty on a person's emotional capacity. In the past, Samantha had spent many months worrying about how she'd pay rent and where the next meal for her family would come from.

"I'm sorry," she said. "These are hard times."

"Not for everyone." Gladys pasted on a smile. "How do you like living with Dr. Higgins? Those apartments on Grover are top-notch."

"It's great. I know I'm fortunate, but I've struggled too. You know that, Gladys." She reached across to pat her friend's arm gently. "Things have a way of working out. They will for you too."

Gladys barely held in a scoff, then changed the subject. "How's the investigation going? Do they know who killed poor Patrick and Bernice yet?"

"Not yet."

Gladys watched Samantha intently as she took another small bite of her sandwich. "Do you think the police are getting close to catching the killer?"

"Yes, I think so. Although, I can't say for sure. I'm doing my own investigation as a journalist, but I don't have the police in my pocket."

"The killer would have to be someone of particular boldness," Gladys said, pushing her untouched bowl of soup to the side, "to pull off two murders in a very public place." Her mouth turned into a strange smile, and she went on as if she wasn't listening anymore. "Someone very cunning."

"It takes someone very evil to take another person's life." Samantha meant to say it with some force, but her voice sounded weak for some reason.

"These are desperate times, though, aren't they?" Gladys cocked her head and looked at Samantha as if she were a strange animal in a cage or a spider in the bathtub.

"I'm . . . uh." Samantha lost her words as a

queasiness overtook her. Blinking rapidly, she tried to focus on Gladys, but one Gladys became two, then one again. Samantha shook her head to clear it and then shakily reached for her glass of water, tipping it over and spilling the remaining contents onto the table. So strange that Gladys didn't make the slightest move to pick it up because Samantha certainly couldn't. In fact, she found she suddenly couldn't move her arms.

"Samantha?"

Samantha's heart beat rapidly in her chest as she struggled for breath.

"Goodbye, Samantha," Gladys said in a sing-song voice that sounded like it was coming from the bottom of a well.

The last thing Samantha registered before the room got dark, and everything went into a desperate silence, was this: Gladys North was the killer.

25

*H*aley punched the receiver button with panicked urgency to find a dial tone and immediately called the operator, demanding to connect to Detective Cluney.

"Please, it's urgent."

"I'll do my best, Dr. Higgins."

After what felt like an interminably long time, she was connected to the precinct, only to be told that the detective wasn't in his office.

"It's about the Baines and Prescott murders. I believe I know who the killer is, and someone's life is in imminent danger. I need a home address for Mr. and Mrs. North."

The officer showed a welcome measure of competence and put another officer on the phone,

Officer Fields, who'd been working this case with Detective Cluney.

"I have all the addresses connected with the suspects, Dr. Higgins; however, this is a matter for the police. I'll send our best men over."

"Officer Fields, it's my good friend's life on the line. You'll give me the address details, or there's a strong chance I'll be seeing your body in the morgue next."

"I'll give it to you, but I'm noting for Detective Cluney's sake that I do so reluctantly."

"You can let me handle Detective Cluney," Haley said, and after Officer Fields had recited the address, she added apologetically, "And I'm sorry for snapping at you. It wasn't very professional."

Before the officer could respond, Haley hung up the phone. Hesitating for a moment, she waited for the dial tone then dialed *The Boston Daily Record.*

"Mr. Milwaukee, please."

In far less time than it had taken for her to be connected to the police, she talked to the debonair reporter.

"Mr. Milwaukee, it's Dr. Haley Higgins."

His smoky voice reached her through the line.

"To what do I owe the pleasure?"

"I'm calling because I'm concerned for the well-being of Miss Hawke."

Mr. Milwaukee's tone grew instantly serious. "Tell me."

"I fear that her friend Mr. North is our killer."

Mr. Milwaukee swore. "She's with Mrs. North now, lunching."

"Yes. Can you meet me there?" She recited the address. "I've called the police, but I don't always have their cooperation."

"You bet."

Haley grabbed her coat and purse, forsaking her hat and gloves, and raced for the door.

"Is there anything I can do to help?" Dr. Martin asked.

"Just hold down the fort here. I'm not sure how long I'll be gone."

Haley headed down Allen Street, cussing at the roundabout way it took to get to the Causeway. Still, once there, she raced past the North Station to the tenement area off Washington and was the first to arrive at the address given to her by Officer Fields. She dashed out into the street, just dodging an angry driver who gave her a warning fist.

Haley shouted an apology then rushed into the building. Forfeiting a polite knock, she tested the knob and found the door unlocked. She flung it open.

The apartment lacked anything that hinted at an effort to make it home, and there was no sign of the Norths.

The scent of soup reached her, rousing her anxiety, and when she entered the kitchen, her heart fell. Sam's arms and head rested on the kitchen table. The rest of her body hung limply in the chair.

"Samantha!"

Haley lifted her friend upright, putting two fingers on her neck in search of a pulse. Finding one, she let out a breath of relief. It was faint, but there.

"Dr. Higgins?"

Haley turned to Johnny's voice. "She's been poisoned. Help me get her to the sink!"

As Johnny propped Samantha up, Haley found a saltshaker, filled a glass with water, and poured a good amount of salt into it.

"You need to drink this, Sam," she said. Holding Samantha's mouth open, she poured the salty water down her throat, happy to see it result in a gagging impulse. "I know it's vile," she said and poured more into Sam's mouth, "but you have to do it."

After a few minutes, Haley got the desired

outcome. Samantha vomited a satisfying amount into the sink.

"We need to get her to the hospital immediately," Haley said. "The Norths don't have a telephone, so it'll be faster just to take my car."

Johnny jumped into play, taking Samantha gently in both arms, one under her shoulders and the other under her knees.

The police pulled up as Johnny awkwardly climbed into the back seat with Sam.

Haley shouted, "The Norths are gone. I'm taking another victim to the hospital. I'd be grateful for an escort."

The trip to the hospital was a lot less frantic with police sirens clearing the way. Haley caught Mr. Milwaukee's worried expression in the rearview mirror.

"Is she going to be okay?" he asked.

"It helps that she expelled her stomach contents." Haley knew that with potent poisons, that wasn't always enough. "Are you a praying man, Mr. Milwaukee?"

"When it suits me."

"You might want to make an appeal now. On my behalf as well, if you don't mind."

When the receptionist at the emergency

entrance saw Dr. Higgins, he immediately came to her aid. "She's been poisoned. I'd appreciate the best doctors and the utmost attention."

"Of course, Dr. Higgins."

Mr. Milwaukee helped to put Samantha on the gurney. To Haley's amazement, Samantha's eyes opened.

"Your prayers seem to have worked, Mr. Milwaukee," Haley said as she took Samantha's hand. "You're going to be all right, Sam. We found you in time."

"Haley," Sam said, her voice weak and ragged. "Mrs. B. . . . cooking . . . roots from Gladys. *It's Gladys.*"

Haley stared at Johnny in horror. She'd gotten it wrong. It wasn't Regis North behind these murders, but his wife. "I've got to go! Please look after Sam until I return."

SCREECHING TO A HALT HAPHAZARDLY, one tire askew on the curb, Haley ran into her building without even bothering to shut the door of her Desoto. Her chest burned as she sprinted past the third-floor entrance, and she vowed to take her physical conditioning more seriously.

Haley found her door unlocked, a common situation in buildings like hers, especially in the daytime hours, which proved that someone was home, and the only person that could be was her neighbor.

"Mrs. Berrymaple!"

The radio in the kitchen was turned up rather loudly to accommodate the woman's gradual hearing loss, and so she didn't seem to make a note of the gravity in Haley's voice. She sang out, "In the kitchen, Dr. Higgins."

Haley nearly skidded around the corner. "Stop!"

Mrs. Berrymaple froze. She was poised over a steaming pot on the gas stove, a spoon in her hand hovering near her mouth.

"Don't eat that," Haley said, forcing calm into her voice. "Put the spoon down and step away from the steam." Haley didn't know if the fumes were poisonous, but she could take no chances.

Mrs. Berrymaple frowned but did as instructed. "Are you quite all right, Dr. Higgins?"

"Have you tasted it already?"

"It's only just thickened enough to bother."

Relieved, Haley moved to the radio on the counter and turned it off. "I don't mean to alarm you, Mrs. Berrymaple, but I believe the soup to be poisoned."

"How is that possible? I cut and peeled the roots myself. Nothing has gone in that pot that I didn't put in it."

"Where did you get the vegetables?"

"Why, they were sitting in the hallway. Didn't you order them?"

"I'm afraid not. And I have worse news. Miss Hawke is in the hospital. The killer got to her, too, but," she added quickly, "she's still alive."

Mrs. Berrymaple reached for the back of a chair to prop herself up. Haley rushed to her side and helped her sit.

"I'd make you some tea, but I really have to go."

"I'll be fine," Mrs. Berrymaple said. "Should I pour out the soup?"

Haley was already putting the lid on it. "I'll keep it in my office, for now, to be tested later." After depositing the pot on her desk, she added over her shoulder, "Please keep the door locked for the time being. And if you don't mind, would you pick Talia up from school?"

"I'd be happy to, Doctor. Anytime. Oh, with all the commotion, I almost forgot. Detective Cluney telephoned. Something about going north by train. I'm sorry, it's hard for me to hear on those contraptions. He repeated the word 'north' a lot, like it was an important point."

Haley had had no idea when she rose that morning that she'd be doing so much running, up and down the stairs no less, and she was winded again when she hopped into her car. It reversed with a clunk when the tire dropped off the curb. She put it into gear and raced to the North Station. Her hunch was right. The Norths were leaving town.

rateful for Detective Cluney's tip, Haley crossed Nashua Street to the west entrance doors of North Station; she quickly checked her watch before hurrying into the busy entrance doors. There were twenty-two tracks in North Station, and although Haley couldn't know exactly which train the Norths intended to board, according to the huge schedule hanging on the wall, there were only four trains set to depart within the next fifteen minutes.

She pivoted back to track number four, the only one with intercity connections, this one to Portland, Maine.

"Dr. Higgins!" Someone called from behind her, and because of the mass of people and the way sound reverberated in the huge building, Haley couldn't immediately place the voice. Scanning the crowd, she found the stocky form of Detective Cluney walking briskly in her direction. There were two younger officers at his wing, one of whom was Officer Fields.

"You got my message," he said in his mild Irish brogue. Slightly out of breath, he stopped to wipe his forehead with a handkerchief. "I had a tail on Regis North, and he let it slip to an informant that he and his missus were skipping town. Since Mrs. North isn't in the best health, I thought it wise to let you tag along."

"It's Gladys North," Haley said as they continued to move through the mass of hurried passengers and past those lounging about with waits ahead of them. "She's the killer."

"Not Regis North? How d'you know that?"

"Gladys tried to kill Samantha Hawke. Sam told me herself."

Haley kept to the front, cutting the trail through the throng, her long legs proving a challenge for the burly detective to keep up with.

"You appear to know where you're going," Detective Cluney remarked.

"I have a hunch they might be northbound on

track number four. It's the only one leaving soon with intercity connections." Haley glanced up at a sign that showed they were on the right path. "I'm aware of family ties in Maine."

"Aha, yes, good thinking."

Several small food establishments were open along the way, and Haley perused each one of them as they passed by. She didn't want to miss the Norths, had they ducked into one of them for a bite to eat. Then, as they passed by a tiny shop selling a somewhat limited selection of baked goods, Haley spotted Regis and Gladys standing at the counter looking over the pastries, each with two suitcases on the floor at their feet.

Haley grabbed Detective Cluney's arm and nodded toward the bakery. "There."

Ensuring the officers could hear him, the detective said, "Don't shout out to stop them. We don't want them to dash off. I don't relish the thought of running pell-mell through these crowds."

The officers cautiously advanced toward the couple, but after only a few steps, Regis North glanced over his shoulder, catching Haley's eye. Regis tapped Gladys's arm while speaking rapidly, and the two picked up their suitcases and ran in the opposite direction, the baker shaking a fist at their failure to pay.

"I don't think they saw you," Haley said. "Let's split up."

Detective Cluney sent his men to circle the other side of the track, stepping in behind Haley as she did her best to keep her eyes on the Norths, matching their quick pace. To overtake them meant she would have to run. One unfortunate collision with one of the hundreds of people making their way through the station could cause Haley to lose sight of the Norths. She kept pace with the couple until they reached their intended departure point.

Taking a position behind a pillar, Haley saw the pensive Norths waiting at track number four. She wanted to make them believe they'd dodged her. The sign above the platform indicated that the train was due to arrive in ten minutes.

"There are my men," Detective Cluney said, "approaching from the other side. We'll box them in."

When the two officers were in position, Haley stepped into view. "Mr. and Mrs. North!"

With shocked expressions, Gladys North grabbed Regis's arm and stared mutely at Haley.

"How d'you find us?" she demanded. "Samantha—"

"Samantha's fine," Haley said, stretching the truth. "I found her in time." She motioned to Detective Cluney, who'd stepped up beside her. "You remember the detective working the homicide of Mr. Baines and Miss Prescott?"

Regis spun on his heel, only to be met with Officer Fields and his partner, who created a barrier. Regis's shoulders dropped as resignation spread to his eyes.

"Gladys North," Detective Cluney began, "you are under arrest for the murder of Patrick Baines and Bernice Prescott and the attempted murder of Mildred Winkley and Samantha Hawke." He produced a set of handcuffs. "Please hold out your hands."

Gladys's face went white as she leaned on her husband for support.

"No, it's me you should be arresting," Regis protested. "I put too much pressure on her. I expected too much. She's with child. Please, I . . . I'm responsible." He held out his wrists.

"We can talk about that later, Mr. North." Detective Cluney looked hard at Gladys, "Right now, I am arresting your wife."

"Ooh." Gladys suddenly held her stomach and bent over.

Haley went to her as she slowly slid to the cement floor with Regis trying to support her.

"My stomach!" Gladys closed her eyes, her face a mask of pain, reassuring Haley that the woman wasn't simply putting on a show.

Detective Cluney stood over her with the handcuffs dangling from his right hand, uncertainty on his face.

Haley knelt on the hard floor and put her hand on Gladys's forehead for a moment. The woman was running a fever, and her eyelids were fluttering. Haley put two fingers on Gladys's neck. Her pulse raced.

"What is it?" Regis demanded.

"I don't know yet, but we'd better get her to the hospital."

"Can she walk?" Detective Cluney said gruffly, putting away the handcuffs.

Haley shook her head. "It's best if we call an ambulance."

"Gladys!" Regis cried as Gladys's chin dropped to her chest and her body went limp.

27

As Samantha's eyelids fluttered open, her eyes fought to focus fully, and her mind grasped to register the unfamiliar surroundings. Where was she, and why was she here?

An image of Talia forced a gasp. Her daughter!

Then, a familiar voice.

"Samantha, doll, it's all right. You're safe."

Through dry lips, she said with a raspy voice, "Johnny?" His face drew closer, his facial features growing crisper. His jaw was tense, and his eyes round with concern.

"You're in the hospital, Sam," he said. "A run-in with a batch of bad soup."

Samantha remembered now. "Gladys?"

"They got her. And her husband too."

"How long have I been here?"

"Three days. You have your good doctor to thank. Her quick thinking saved your life." A grin crossed his handsome face. "Though it was mighty disgusting to watch."

"I . . . vomited?"

After a chortle, Johnny said, "Enough to fill a washtub."

Samantha swallowed. No wonder her throat hurt, along with her pride. She must be a mess. Three days without bathing, and she didn't even want to know how toilet needs had been tended to. And here was Johnny, clean-shaven, smelling like Williams Aqua Velva, and a witness to her explosion of vomit; she couldn't feel any smaller.

"Hey?" he said. "Are you all right? Do I need to fetch a nurse?"

"No," Samantha said wearily. "I wouldn't mind a bit of water, though."

A ceramic pitcher sat on a counter, and Johnny used it to pour a glass of water, then handed it to her. It wasn't until the water hit her lips that she realized how parched she was. She gulped like the proverbial man in the desert oasis.

"Whoa, partner," Johnny said with a laugh. "There's more where that came from."

Samantha wiped the dampness from her chin with her hand, then patted at her hair with the excess. "Why are you here?" she finally asked.

"I'll try not to be offended," Johnny said lightly.

"I just mean, why not Haley or Mrs. Berrymaple?"

"You actually just missed the good doctor, Sleeping Beauty. We've been doing shifts. This is mine."

"Again, why you?"

"Why not me? We're friends, right? Work colleagues, at least. Besides, the pit is unbearable without you there. It's amazing how the presence of a lady restrains the despicable beastliness of men that surfaces when they are gathered together without one."

Samantha smiled. "I'd better get back there as soon as I can."

"I couldn't agree more. But to be fair to the fellows, they did send you this." Johnny pulled a small rectangular box from his pocket. "It's not much, so don't get too excited. It's a token."

Samantha received the box and tentatively

opened it. She couldn't guess what the pit crew would've bought for her, and she couldn't conceal her surprise when she saw it. Her gaze darted to Johnny.

"A Parker Parco fountain pen?" Samantha had never owned such a premium writing utensil. She admired its green marble-like finish.

"It's engraved, see? 'Reporter Samantha Hawke.'" Johnny leaned back casually in the wooden chair provided for visitors, his hands shoved in his pockets. "Like I said, a token."

"It's more than a token, Johnny. And I'm delighted. Please thank them until I can do so myself."

Johnny offered a nod, and Samantha watched him from under her eyelashes. Now that she knew about his past, that he wasn't the selfish narcissist that she'd thought, but a man who'd put up barriers in carefree nonchalance to protect his heart, Samantha's feelings for him grew fonder.

Except, she could never let him know she knew, and especially how she knew.

It was best if she didn't open her heart to him too much.

"How's Talia?" she asked, changing the subject.

She knew her daughter's physical needs would be taken care of by Haley and Mrs. Berrymaple, but her concern was for Talia's emotional needs. "This must be very confusing and frightening for her."

"They haven't let her in the hospital yet," he said. "They wanted to wait until you were awake." He sat up. "Would you like me to give your doctor a call?"

"In a moment. First, can you tell me what happened? The last thing I remember is losing focus on Gladys's face just as I put it together that she was the killer."

"Your Dr. Higgins figured it out, though at first, she thought it was Regis North who did the dastardly deeds. When she couldn't reach you, she called me. We arrived separately at the North residence at the same time . . ." His voice hitched. "When I saw you passed out, well, it was an awful moment for both of us. Dr. Higgins found a pulse and went to work drowning you in salt water. Like I said, you left a mess in the sink."

Samantha was about to protest, but when Johnny took her hand, she lost her words.

"It's all right, doll," he said gently. "Rest now. And I'll see what I can do about bringing in your little girl."

. . .

THE LAST THREE days had been a blur. The arrest of Gladys North on murder charges and Regis North on aiding and abetting headlined all the newspapers. Justice for Patrick Baines and Bernice Prescott would be granted, and praise for Haley's involvement and her cooperation with the police had the morgue telephone ringing off the hook.

Which was why she was working from her office at home. At any rate, Haley reserved her comments, giving them to Johnny Milwaukee exclusively, with the provision he shared the byline with Samantha, something he agreed to do without reservation.

While Regis North was behind bars, Gladys remained in the hospital under police protection. Sadly, Gladys's attempt at ending her pregnancy had worked, if belatedly, and the child was lost soon after her arrest at the train station. She confessed drying the water hemlock, grinding it to dust, and dissolving it in water. She'd picked it at her in-laws' farm in Maine and replanted in their balcony garden box—intending to kill off her opponents. Regis had explained the toxicity of the plant to her, not realizing he'd seeded the idea for Gladys's revenge.

Gladys carried her poisoned concoction in a small vial, adding drops to a water cup before filling it, giving one to Patrick Baines when she was still a contestant and they shared a water break, and then again to Bernice Prescott when Gladys had offered to assist the nurses. It turned out that the mishap Mrs. Sikes had had with her water, spilling it on her dress instead of drinking it, had saved her life. Miss Prescott was targeted out of jealousy and animosity, which had caused Gladys, in her growing derangement, to lose sight of the fact that if Miss Prescott were eliminated, so would Regis be.

Having revived enough to tell her story, Nurse Winkley stated that Gladys North had come to her to ask for help to end her pregnancy, which the nurse had refused to give. During this visit, Gladys had spitefully poisoned the stew when Mildred Winkley wasn't looking.

Haley suspected Gladys North would be spared the noose and sentenced to time in an insane asylum, as a case for mental incompetence would be strong.

Gladys's accusations of cheating by the Sikeses had reached the tabloids, resulting in a search of the Sikes's residence and their subsequent arrest. Mr. Sikes pled not guilty. He threw the blame onto his ex-wife, claiming she was the one with the addiction. Haley believed him, though his behavior toward his former wife was ungentlemanly.

Mr. Farber, guilty of nothing more than greed

and callousness, called their win foul and was now demanding a return of the prize money.

Haley's mind went to Samantha. Was she still unconscious? She had to put her faith in the doctors who were confident that she'd pull through in time. Haley inhaled deeply, finding reassurance in her medical colleagues' prognosis.

Thinking of medical colleagues brought Gerald and Dr. Murphy to mind. Haley blushed with shame at her childish response to a handsome face. On hearing about her involvement in solving this case, Dr. Murphy had come to the morgue, but not before Haley had seen him flirting with a pretty nurse in the hall. She'd thanked him for taking time to congratulate her, then politely dismissed him, using her pile of paperwork as an excuse.

Gerald had agreed to return to their previous platonic understanding, enjoying each other's company at public events, removing any expectation to private affairs.

At least for now.

The telephone rang, and Haley quickly picked it up, knowing that only news of Samantha's well-being was to be directed to this line.

"Hello?"

It was Johnny Milwaukee on the line.

"She's awake and wants to see you."

Haley gripped her heart, relieved. "Thank goodness. We're on our way."

She rushed to the kitchen, where Mrs. Berrymaple and Talia sat at the table, working on a jigsaw puzzle. Mr. Midnight watched from the window perch.

"Get your coat, Talia," Haley said. "I have good news. We're going to visit your mommy."

If you enjoyed reading Death by Dancing *please help others enjoy it too.*

Recommend it: *Help others find the book by recommending it to friends, readers' groups, and discussion boards.*

Suggest it *to your local librarian.*

Review it: *Please tell other readers why you liked this book by reviewing it at your point of purchase.*

** Please do not use spoilers in your review**

Don't miss the next Higgins & Hawke mystery!

DEATH ON TREMONT ROW
A Higgins & Hawke Mystery #5

Death is greatly depressing!

IT'S BEEN five years since Haley Higgins she moved back from London to Boston, and in that time she'd become a doctor of pathology and the assistant pathologist at the Boston City Morgue. In her position she often assists in the solving of crimes and murders, particularly since she's been working in tandem with Samantha Hawke, an intrepid newspaper reporter and good friend.

In the spring of 1932, depression is widespread in all its forms. Haley is cheered by news that her good friend Ginger Reed, also known as Lady Gold and a former resident of Boston, is coming to visit! Naturally, Ginger will want to spend time with her sister and stepmother, but there will certainly be time for two old friends to chum around.

Tremont Row, a bustling shopping and theatre district, is exactly the kind of place Haley and Ginger, along with Samantha, love to hang out. Until a stabbing death interferes with their shopping plans!

Haley and Samantha, continuing to fight the patriarchal barriers in their respective fields, work together to find justice for the latest victim. Is it a crime driven by the desperation of poverty, or is the motive far more sinister?

Shop at leestraussbooks.com

New 1950s Ginger Gold spin-off series! Meet Miss Rosa Reed!

MURDER AT HIGH TIDE
A Rosa Reed Mystery #1

Murder's all wet!

IT'S 1956 and WPC (Woman Police Constable) Rosa Reed has left her groom at the altar in London.

Time spent with her American cousins in Santa Bonita, California is exactly what she needs to get back on her feet, though the last thing she expected was to get entangled in another murder case!

When a body floats onto the beach at a charity event hosted by Rosa's Aunt Louisa, Rosa's detective instincts kick in. Can she help solve the case and save her aunt's reputation? Even if it means working with her old flame, Detective Miguel Belmonte?

If you love early rock & roll, poodle skirts, clever who-dun-its, a charming cat and an even more charming detective, you're going to love this new series!

Shop at leestraussbooks.com

For information on the next new releases and deals, be sure to sign up for Lee's newsletter!

MURDER *on the* SS *Rosa* is where we first meet Haley Higgins. If you haven't started the Ginger Gold Mystery series, now's your chance!

Murder's a pain in the bow!

It's 1923 and bright young thing Ginger Gold makes a cross-Atlantic journey from Boston to London, England. When the ship's captain is found dead in a most intriguing fashion, Ginger is only too happy to lend her assistance to the handsome Chief Inspector Basil Reed.

This fun, jazz-age whodunit has readers saying "Lady Gold is a charming heroine" and "can't stop reading!"

Murder on the SS Rosa will have you laughing, crying, and guessing until the last page.

Get started and download the first book in this binge-worthy series today.

Shop at leestraussbooks.com

ABOUT THE AUTHOR

Lee Strauss is a USA TODAY bestselling author of The Ginger Gold Mysteries series, The Higgins & Hawke Mystery series, The Rosa Reed Mystery series (cozy historical mysteries), A Nursery Rhyme Mystery series (mystery suspense), The Light & Love series (sweet romance), The Clockwise Collection (YA time travel romance), and young adult historical fiction with over a million books read. She has titles published in German and French, and a growing audio library.

When Lee's not writing or reading she likes to cycle, hike, and stare at the ocean. She loves to drink caffè lattes and red wines in exotic places, and eat dark chocolate anywhere.

For more info on books by Lee Strauss and her social media links, visit leestraussbooks.com. To make sure you don't miss the next new release, be sure to sign up for her readers' list!

Discuss the books, ask questions, share your opinions. Fun giveaways! Join the Lee Strauss Readers' Group on Facebook for more info.

Love the fashions of the 1920s? Check out Ginger Gold's Pinterest Board!

Did you know you can follow your favourite authors on Bookbub? If you subscribe to Bookbub — (and if you don't, why don't you? - They'll send you daily emails alerting you to sales and new releases on just the kind of books you like to read!) — follow me to make sure you don't miss the next Ginger Gold Mystery!

BB Follow on BookBub

g follow me on
goodreads

www.leestraussbooks.com

leestraussbooks@gmail.com

HIGGINS & HAWKE MYSTERY SERIES (cozy 1930s historical)

The 1930s meets Rizzoli & Isles in this friendship depression era cozy mystery series.

Death at the Tavern

Death on the Tower

Death on Hanover

Death by Dancing

Death on Tremont Row

GINGER GOLD MYSTERY SERIES (cozy 1920s historical)

Cozy. Charming. Filled with Bright Young Things. This Jazz Age murder mystery will entertain and delight you with its 1920s flair and pizzazz!

Murder on the SS Rosa

Murder at Hartigan House

Murder at Bray Manor

Murder at Feathers & Flair

Murder at the Mortuary

Murder at Kensington Gardens

Murder at St. George's Church

The Wedding of Ginger & Basil

Murder Aboard the Flying Scotsman

Murder at the Boat Club

Murder on Eaton Square

Murder by Plum Pudding

Murder on Fleet Street

Murder at Brighton Beach

Murder in Hyde Park

Murder at the Royal Albert Hall

Murder in Belgravia

Murder on Mallowan Court

Murder at the Savoy

Murder at the Circus

LADY GOLD INVESTIGATES (Ginger Gold companion short stories)

Volume 1

Volume 2

A NURSERY RHYME MYSTERY SERIES(mystery/sci fi)

Marlow finds himself teamed up with intelligent and savvy Sage Farrell, a girl so far out of his league he feels blinded in her presence - literally - damned glasses! Together they work to find the identity of @gingerbreadman. Can they stop the killer before he strikes again?

Gingerbread Man

Life Is but a Dream

Hickory Dickory Dock

Twinkle Little Star

LIGHT & LOVE (sweet romance)

Set in the dazzling charm of Europe, follow Katja, Gabriella, Eva, Anna and Belle as they find strength, hope and love.

Love Song

Your Love is Sweet

In Light of Us

Lying in Starlight

PLAYING WITH MATCHES (WW2 history/romance)

A sobering but hopeful journey about how one young German boy copes with the war and propaganda. Based on true events.

A Piece of Blue String (companion short story)

THE CLOCKWISE COLLECTION (YA time travel romance)

Casey Donovan has issues: hair, height and uncontrollable trips to the 19th century! And now this ∼ she's accidentally taken Nate Mackenzie, the cutest boy in the school, back in time. Awkward.

Clockwise

Clockwiser

Like Clockwork

Counter Clockwise

Clockwork Crazy

Clocked (companion novella)

<u>Standalones</u>

Seaweed

Love, Tink